Show Me

Sharon C. Cooper

ISBN: 978-1-946172-25-9

Disclaimer

DEAR READER

It's always a pleasure hooking up with some of my author friends to bring you a fabulous collaboration! Me, Sheryl Lister and Delaney Diamond present to you the *Irresistible Husband Series*! SHOW ME is my contribution, and I can't wait for you to meet Colton (Cole) and Malaya.

Brace yourself. You're in for a special treat with this series!

Enjoy!

Sharon C. Cooper

NOTE: The *Irresistible Husband Series* can be read in any order.

CHAPTER ONE

"You guys are idiots. Axel, you're too withdrawn and emotionally unavailable to women. Though you make jokes, it's probably because of how your engagement ended. Braxton, you're waiting for a *perfect* woman. She doesn't exist because no one is perfect. If you stopped being so picky, you might find someone. And you, my dear brother, are the most self-centered man to walk the face of the earth. You guys are never going to marry anyone until you make some changes."

Colton Eubanks loosened his tie and half-listened to his sister, Dani. He had arrived at Double Trouble, a bar they owned together, a few minutes ago to have a drink with a couple of his friends. What he hadn't expected was for her to go on and on telling them why they weren't marriage material. He hated they even brought up the topic.

"What makes you the authority on why we aren't married and won't, according to you, ever get married?" Cole asked.

"The three of you come in here at least once a week griping about this woman or that woman. I listen, and it's the same complaints every time. You think someone is always after your money or trying to use you in some way," she said to Cole. "And Axel, the way you go through women, how is it possible you haven't found anyone yet? Could it be because you refuse to open up? As for you, Braxton, before you say you're not *that* picky, trust me—you are."

Cole sipped his scotch to hide a smile. She was right about his two buddies, but she had him all wrong. He wasn't self-centered or selfish, another adjective she usually used when referring to him. He might've had some self-serving tendencies, but he wasn't one of those men who only thought about himself. He was very giving…to those who were deserving. As far as Cole was concerned, though, people, especially women, were always trying to get something from him, and he wasn't having it.

Okay, maybe he *was* a little selfish in that regard.

Cole watched his sister saunter to the other end of the bar to fix a drink for a newcomer. Dani was two years younger than him, but since they were kids, she always acted as if she was the oldest.

"You think Dani is right?" Braxton asked, pulling Cole out of his thoughts.

He, Axel, and Braxton were huddled at the far end of the bar near the servers' station. They'd first met years ago when playing on a basketball league. Since then, they'd become close friends, and their weekly drink at the bar gave them a chance to catch up with each other.

"Serious about which part?" Cole asked him, even though he was fairly sure he knew what Braxton was really asking.

"About me being too picky."

Cole nodded. "Yeah, I think her assessment was right, but I don't see anything wrong with being choosy. You want what you want. There's nothing wrong with that. Don't let my sister get inside your head," Cole insisted, though he should probably take his own advice.

The problem with Dani's want-to-be-a-therapist assessments was that most of the time she was right. And unfortunately, they would all probably obsess about her depiction of them for the next few days. There was just something about Dani. She had the uncanny ability to get under your skin like an irritating splinter, making you painfully aware that it's there, but not easy to dig out. In Dani's case, she just bugged the heck out of Cole.

"You're right." Braxton took a long drag on his beer and slammed the bottle onto the bar top. "Ain't nothing wrong with being picky and holding out for the right woman."

"Nope, nothing wrong with it at all," Axel agreed with finality. "And I'm not emotionally withdrawn. Hell, is that even a thing? Ain't nothing wrong with me taking my time before I leap again. I know the type of woman I want, and I know she's out there."

Cole and his friends were ready to find Miss Right and settle down and have a family; him especially. He had just celebrated his thirty-ninth birthday a few weeks ago, reminding him that he was behind schedule with his life plan. By thirty-five, he was supposed to be firmly set into his investment management career, own real estate around the country, and be financially secure. All of that was in place.

By forty, though, the plan was to be married and have at least one child. At the moment he wasn't even dating. So, accomplishing that goal was going to be impossible…unless a certain someone started taking his interest in her seriously. *Malaya Radcliff.*

Cole's gaze sought her out, and he spotted her as she strolled from the back of the bar, carrying a tray of food to a booth. Double Trouble wasn't a full-service restaurant, but they did have a grill and served sandwiches, fries, onion rings, chips, and dip, along with a few other snack items.

His attention stayed on Malaya. She only worked at the bar part-time, but they'd gotten to know each other pretty well over the past year. He liked everything about the woman, especially the way his body stirred whenever she was in his line of sight.

Malaya smiled at the man and woman she was serving, and just like that, Cole's exhausting day was almost forgotten. That's the affect she had on him. Too bad she wasn't interested in anything more than friendship. She was focused and working toward accomplishing her own life goals and even at thirty-four, that didn't include a romantic relationship.

What a shame.

Cole already knew, based on their interactions, that they'd be great together. They both enjoyed sports, loved to laugh, and even liked the same movies. More than that, the attraction crackling between them couldn't be denied by either of them. Still, she wouldn't give him a chance. He had asked her out on more than one occasion, but each time, she graciously said no. It wasn't that she wasn't interested in him. Cole had it on good authority that Malaya was feelin' him the moment they'd met. At least according to Dani.

Surprisingly, his sister actually thought that they'd make a great couple. It was shocking because Dani and Malaya were friends, and Dani used to threaten bloody murder if Cole even looked at any of her girlfriends.

Cole's gaze latched on to Malaya as she approached the bar with the large round tray under her arm. Like usual, an overwhelming sense of rightness surrounded him. He couldn't explain it, but it happened whenever she was near. Like she was already a part of him. Maybe it was in his head, or just maybe she really was the woman of his dreams.

Malaya set the tray down and leaned against the bar next to Cole. The clang of silver bangles and bracelets on her left wrist jingled with every move she made. Someone could probably hear her coming from a block away. She wore just that many.

"How's it going, fellas?" she asked.

"All is well except Dani giving us a hard time," Axel said and caught Malaya up to speed on parts of the conversation they'd been having.

Cole took that opportunity to check her out. He loved her style, which was different from those he usually dated. Malaya had a seventies vibe about her, including an afro, a colorful shirt, and tonight, even bell bottom jeans. Her daily fashion also included ear piercings—six in one ear and three in the other. From day one, he'd been curious about whether or not she had any other piercings on her body. If he was lucky, who knew…maybe he'd find out.

He continued studying her while she chatted with Axel and Braxton. Malaya was sweet, tough, and fiercely independent, all rolled into one beautiful package.

"How ya doin'? You look a little tired," Cole said to her when the guys started discussing the basketball game that was playing on the TV behind the bar. "Did you have classes today?"

"Boy, did I. I had three classes and two of those included exams. Add that to my three hours of sleep last night, and you have a person operating on fumes right now."

She gave a little laugh and rubbed the back of her neck. While working two part-time jobs, she had also returned to school to finish her degree. Some days, Cole didn't know how she did it, but she rarely complained about her busy schedule.

"Hey, sweetie. How about another beer?" a guy on the other side of the room yelled.

Malaya squeezed Cole's arm as she pushed away from the bar. "Duty calls, but first," she leaned in and placed a lingering kiss on his cheek, "thank you for the flowers," she whispered. "I know they were from you."

Cole's pulse sped up. If a little peck on the cheek had his body responding like that, what would happen if he got the opportunity to taste her tempting lips? She'd had a rough couple of days with school and juggling work, and he'd had flowers delivered to the bar earlier. He hadn't signed his name on the card, but wrote: *Hang in there.*

While Malaya crossed to her customers, the gentle sway of her hips was almost hypnotizing as her confident walk carried her to the other side of the room. Man, she was the total package. He had to figure out a way to get her to take him seriously about dating. It was risky asking an employee out, but since Cole wasn't her immediate supervisor, he didn't see anything wrong with it.

Besides, he only stopped in once or twice a week to have a drink and take care of the bar's books. The only thing standing in their way—well, at least one thing—was that Dani had told him that Malaya thought he was outside of her league.

Cole shook his head and took another sip of his drink. Whether he was or not, he wanted the chance to see if their chemistry was as strong as it seemed to be. Malaya was the type of woman he wanted permanently in his life. He just had to figure out a way to make that happen.

*

The pouring rain and the light breeze outside of the bar's covered back deck would've normally relaxed Malaya. Not tonight. Her angry footsteps pounded the hardwood as she paced the length of the deck that was connected to the bar. She fumed with every word her ex-husband spoke. She hated calling him for any reason, but for her daughter, Destiny, there was nothing she wouldn't do. Even put up with her jerk of an ex.

She hadn't intended to tell him that she was planning to seek sole custody, but somehow, the words slipped through her lips. Now she had to listen to him go on and on about why she was an unfit parent. At least too unfit, in his opinion, to care for Destiny.

"You will *never* get custody of our daughter. Do you hear me? I don't care what type of dime-store lawyer you find. Destiny's not going anywhere. You're lucky I even let you have her every other weekend and holidays."

"You don't *let* me. I see her then because that's what the court ordered," Malaya snapped.

There she went again, opening her mouth. She could only attribute her lack of patience to being tired. It was almost ten o'clock, and she'd been up since four o'clock that morning. Exhaustion didn't even describe the unwavering weariness that had seeped into her bones and settled there. She could barely see straight, let alone think rationally.

The worst part? Once she finished her shift at the bar, she still had to work on a paper that was due for one of her classes on Monday.

It'll all pay off in the long run, she reminded herself. Everything she was doing, every sacrifice she was making, was for her baby girl.

"She's staying right here with me. You might as well give up on any crazy ideas flowing through your head."

Malaya listened as Todd continued talking about how their ten-year-old daughter preferred living with him and his wife, Selena. Malaya knew better. She might only get to see Destiny every other weekend, but no one knew her child better than she did. Destiny was old enough to say who she wanted to live with, and it wasn't with Todd and his trifling wife.

What made the whole situation even worse was that Todd didn't really want custody of Destiny. Sure, he loved their daughter in his own way, but her needs weren't his priority. He and his wife traveled more than they stayed home, and Destiny was often left with a nanny or their housekeeper. She was like a trophy to Todd. He got to show her off to all of his wealthy friends and play the doting father whenever it suited him.

Malaya didn't care what it took, soon he wouldn't be able to use their daughter for his own twisted delusion of proper parenting. When Todd gained sole custody, there had been so many factors against Malaya. The whole situation had caught her off guard, and she had so many regrets. The biggest? Not fighting harder. She just never thought a judge would rule in Todd's favor. To this day, Malaya believed he paid off the judge. She just couldn't prove it. With Todd and his family's money, there wasn't much he didn't get away with. It hadn't helped that her incompetent lawyer had been a joke, but at the time, she hadn't been able to afford a better one.

"For years you depended on me and still you can barely take care of yourself," Todd's rant continued. "How are you going to be able to afford a preteen? Destiny has a certain lifestyle that she's accustomed to. You'll never be able to give her what I can give to her."

Anger boiled inside of Malaya. He didn't know her. She wasn't the young, impressionable girl she used to be when he and she first met. Now she was independent and slowly pulling her life together. Todd might have more money, but Malaya planned to fight him with every single penny she had. Destiny was depending on her.

"And if you keep threatening to take my child away from me, I'll take her so far away from Georgia, you'll never see her again."

Fear and rage warred within Malaya. He'd been threatening to do just that for the past year. Usually she'd back off and play nice, but not this time.

"Let me talk to her," Malaya demanded. The bar had gotten busy and time had gotten away from her. Otherwise she would've called earlier. It wasn't until a few minutes ago that Malaya realized Destiny had tried calling her.

"It's after ten, and she's asleep. A good mother would know that."

"I need to talk to her!" Malaya huffed out a breath, willing herself to calm down. She knew from experience that she would never get anywhere with him by demanding anything. "Please, Todd. I need to talk to my daughter," she said, the fight seeping out of her.

Todd didn't respond.

"Hello? Todd? Hello!" Malaya yelled before pulling the phone from her ear and glancing at the screen.

He had hung up.

Frustration roared through her body like a vicious storm and she gripped the cell phone tighter. It was all she could do to keep from chucking it across the deck.

Exhaling unsteadily, she brought the device to her chest and slammed her eyes closed. The rain was coming down harder and a chill crept into her bones. She couldn't let Todd win. Yet, it was getting harder to control her anger when it came to him.

Most days, Malaya felt helpless and tired. Tired of Todd dictating what she could and couldn't do as it related to their daughter. Tired of having to fight for everything, and tired of struggling to create a better life for herself.

"Laya?"

Malaya jerked, startled by the sound of Cole's deep voice. A tear slipped from her eye and she quickly swiped it away before turning to him. He was the last person she wanted to see her crying.

He stood in the doorway that led back into the bar, concern glimmering in his light-brown eyes. Just the sight of him made her heart beat a little faster. Her gaze slowly traveled down his six-foot muscular stature and worked its way back up.

The past year, Cole had been letting his hair grow out. The look made her think of the R&B singer, Maxwell, back in the early 2000s. The big hair and his handsome golden-brown skin were similar. Malaya loved a man with a little scruff on his face, and Cole's perfectly kempt facial hair made her want to run her hands over his cheeks and chin.

Was his hair as soft as it appeared?

Her attention went lower, sweeping across his wide chest and broad shoulders. He had long since shed his suit jacket and tie, leaving him in a deep gray dress shirt and perfectly tailored pants.

"What's wrong?" he asked, stepping onto the deck.

Immediately, his intoxicating scent, a mixture of cedar wood and vanilla, carried on a breeze and wrapped around her like a loving embrace. Cole was downright *fine* and always smelled good. Add that to his intelligent mind, kind and easygoing demeanor, and his successful life, and you had the man of her dreams.

"I heard you yelling. Is everything okay?"

He had probably been in the office working late. It was only a few feet from the back door.

"I'm sorry I disturbed you. It's just..." She was sick of talking about her ex-husband. Cole knew a little about her situation, but not everything.

"Let me guess. Todd again," he said.

Malaya nodded, suddenly too emotional to say anything. Some days she felt as if she was going to crumble like tiny shards of glass. This was one of those days. It was so hard to stay encouraged and continue moving forward when she felt as if her whole life was a losing battle.

When would it get better? When would some of the

weight lighten?

Cole moved closer and wrapped his arms around her. Malaya shivered against him and didn't have the energy to pull away. Actually, she didn't want to. She needed a hug more than she cared to admit.

Still holding tight to her cell phone, she looped her arms around Cole's waist and laid her head on his chest. He placed a kiss against her temple, and Malaya released a soft sigh. It didn't matter how pissed she was at Todd, or how exhausting her day had been, Cole had a way of making her feel better.

"What can I do to help?" His voice was gentle, yet powerful.

He was such an amazing man. There wasn't much he couldn't do. There'd been times when she wanted to go to him for advice on how to best deal with her ex, but Malaya was determined to handle her problems herself. For years, she'd depended on Todd, and he had been good at enabling her.

Since then, she worked hard to become her own person. Changing her dependent behavior was one of the toughest things she'd ever done. She struggled each and every day. It was an ongoing battle, but a battle she intended to win. That meant standing on her own two feet and relying on herself.

"The hug is helping more than you'll ever know," she finally said against Cole's crisp shirt.

God, it felt good to be in his arms. It would be so easy to just stay right where she was, hugged up against his hard body and soaking up some of his positive energy. Unfortunately, she had tables to tend to and drinks to serve.

She pulled slowly out of his hold. "Thanks for the hug. I needed it."

"Anytime you need one, you know where to find me."

That brought a smile to Malaya's face. "You're such a good friend," she said, then regretted her words the moment he frowned. He'd made it clear, more than once, that he didn't want to be just friends. "I mean…more than a friend," she hurried to say.

She would love to pursue an intimate relationship with

Cole. She'd been in lust with him from the moment they'd met. But the two of them as a couple wasn't in the stars. Cole was established and settled, while she was still trying to make sense of her life.

What did she have to offer? Nothing but baggage. But if by chance a fairy godmother happened to appear holding a magic wand and grant Malaya two wishes, one would be used on Destiny. The other...Malaya would wish for Cole to be her man.

"Well, I guess I'll have to settle for *more than a friend,*" Cole said, his words breaking into Malaya's thoughts. "As your friend, though, if you ever need me, I'm here for you. Okay?"

Malaya nodded. "I know, and I don't know what I'd do without you and Dani. You guys gave me a job when I needed it most, even though I didn't have much experience. I've learned so much from both of you. You're like family to me."

"We feel the same way about you."

"Hey!" Dani yelled from the doorway, her hands on her hips. "What are you guys doing out here? I can't run this place by myself. One of y'all better get in here and help."

"I know. I'm sorry. I'm coming," Malaya said, and glanced at Cole as she backed toward the door. "Thank you...for everything."

She rushed past Dani feeling much better than when she'd first gone outside. Like so many times before, Cole had given her that boost she needed.

Who knew—maybe one day they could be a couple and explore a romantic relationship.

A girl can dream.

CHAPTER TWO

"If you hurt her, I will kill you," Dani said through gritted teeth while pointing at Cole. She had stepped out onto the back deck, giving him one of her evil glares. "I'm serious. Laya has been through too much already. Don't play with her."

Playing with Malaya was the last thing Cole wanted to do, at least in the way his sister was referring to. He wanted to love on her. He wanted to be the man she turned to whenever she needed a shoulder to cry on or a listening ear.

Seeing how protective Dani was being reminded him of when they were kids. She always looked out for the underdogs, making it her business to defend and elevate them. Apparently, that hadn't changed.

Cole glanced around the empty deck and slipped a piece of cinnamon gum into his mouth. He thought better when he was chewing. "First of all, I was just comforting Malaya because of something her loser ex-husband said or did," Cole explained. "Secondly, I would never hurt her, and you know that."

"I know you wouldn't intentionally hurt her, but I also know you're attracted to her. Don't be trying to lead Laya on if you're not serious about her, Cole. She's not like those bougie women you tend to gravitate to. She's vulnerable."

"I don't date *bougie* women."

As a matter of fact, Cole couldn't stand fake women who acted as if they were all that. Sure, he had picked a couple of duds, but those relationships never lasted. Dani jammed her hands onto her hips. "Seriously? You're going to stand there and say that to me with a straight face? Have you forgotten about gold-digger Angela? Or what about *I-need-you-like-I-need-air* Melissa?" Cole hadn't forgotten either of them. Angela was out to land either a sugar daddy or at least someone who could afford her extravagant spending habits. And Melissa had tried on more than one occasion to infiltrate his life and move into his house. She had even lied about being homeless, when, in fact, she'd been living with another man. Those were two instances when he had allowed a woman's outer beauty to overshadow their inner ugliness. That wasn't a conversation he wanted to get into with his sister.

"In regard to what you walked in on out here, all I did was offer to help Malaya with whatever is going on. Like usual, she said 'thanks, but no thanks.' So why don't you tell me what's up with her? She's not the wilting flower type, but she's been a little...emotional, for lack of a better word. I'm pretty sure the problem has to do with Todd."

Dani didn't say anything right away, then huffed out a breath. She glanced back at the door to the bar before returning her attention to Cole. "Get her to tell you, but it has to do with Destiny."

Cole frowned and a wave of possessiveness slammed through him. Not only was he crazy about Malaya, but if he ever had a daughter, he'd want her to be just like Destiny. Sweet, spunky, and cute, she reminded him so much of her mother.

"Is Destiny all right? Did Todd do something?" Cole bit out, his hands reflexively fisted at his sides.

"No. He's his usual jerk-wad self. Laya is just sick of having to go through him for anything pertaining to their daughter."

Cole relaxed his stance and unclenched his hands. There

was so much he didn't know about that situation. "How did he even get custody of Destiny in the first place?"

Dani lifted her hands out in front of her. "That's not my story to tell. I've already said too much. Anything else you want to know, talk to Malaya." Dani turned to go back into the building, but stopped. "Cole, if there is anything you can do to help her, I hope you will." With that, she was gone.

What the heck was that supposed to mean?

*

Monday morning Cole trudged into his office, still thinking about Malaya and his conversation with Dani. For much of the weekend, he'd been wondering how he could help Malaya if she wasn't willing to talk to him. He'd tried again when they locked up the bar Friday night, but still, she claimed it was her problem to deal with.

Cole set his laptop on his desk and glanced up when a soft knock sounded on his office door.

"Hey, Valerie. How's your morning going?"

She came further into the office, holding a computer tablet. "It was going great until I realized I goofed up one of your appointments."

Valerie had been with the company for fifteen years and had been his assistant for six of those years. Cole didn't even want to think about how his work life would be without her.

"Did you do something different with your hair?" he asked. She was in her late fifties but was trendier than most women her age. She was always trying something different. Like now, her hair was in elaborate twists that stopped just above her shoulders in a bob-like style.

"Cole, I love you," she said seriously, holding the tablet to her chest while gazing at him as if she really did love him. He knew that wasn't possible, because she was crazy about her husband of thirty years.

Cole sat in his desk chair. "I love you, too, but why do I have the feeling that Jeremiah screwed up somehow?" he said of her husband.

"Do you know, that man didn't notice my hair until I was

leaving for work this morning? Mind you, I got it done yesterday evening. We ate dinner together. Watched TV together. Heck, we even shared the same bed. Not once did he say anything about my hair. At least not until this morning."

Cole laughed. "Maybe he had a lot on his mind."

"Oh, please. I do everything. He ain't got nothin' on his mind. But anyway, enough about me." She came around the desk and set the tablet in front of him, pointing at his busy schedule that was on the screen. "Somehow, I managed to double-book you, but don't worry, I fixed the problem. The only thing is, your day is going to be a little longer this evening."

Since Cole didn't have anyone to go home to, he was used to working late. The rare occasions he did leave early was if he were needed at the bar, or his family needed him for something.

"That's not a problem. I don't have any plans this evening."

Loud cheers sounded in the hallway near Cole's office door, and he glanced at Valerie. She might've been his assistant, but she always knew everything that was going on in the office.

"That's probably Thomas letting everyone know that he and Jessica are expecting their first child. He mentioned it to me when he arrived this morning." She had barely got the last sentence out when Thomas appeared at the door.

"Hey! Did Valerie tell you my good news?"

Cole stood and walked around his desk to shake his coworker's hand.

"She did. Congratulations, man," Cole said around the lump in his throat. He really was happy for Thomas and his wife, but a little pang of jealousy pierced Cole's chest. It seemed every week their office was celebrating one life-changing event after another. Last week, Eric and his wife celebrated their first anniversary. The other week, Ted's oldest daughter gave birth to his first grandchild. Besides him, and out of twenty managers, there was only one other person not engaged or married.

"Thanks, we're pretty hyped. We weren't really trying, but we weren't *not* trying either." Thomas grinned and it was impossible not to be happy for the guy. "You know, man. I think you might be the only one around here still holding on to the bachelor's life. You're not getting any younger. It might be time for you to hang it up and joined the married club."

Cole nodded, unsure of what to say.

Valerie waved Thomas off. "Don't rush him. He'll get there in his own time."

"Yeah, you're probably right." Thomas glanced at his watch. "Let me get to my office. I have a meeting in a few minutes. Oh, but a few of us are going out for lunch to celebrate. You two are more than welcome to join us."

"I would, but I already have plans," Cole said, even though he didn't. He'd find somewhere to go or something to do during that time. It might've been a punk move, but he wasn't in the mood for celebrating.

"I can't make it either, but congratulations again," Valerie added.

"Thanks. See you guys later."

Cole closed the door behind Thomas and reclaimed his seat. He didn't have to look at Valerie to know that she was staring at him. He could feel her gaze clawing into the side of his face.

"Is there anything else I need to know about the day?" he asked as he booted up his computer.

"You know," Valerie started and headed to the door, "a friend of mine has a daughter that I think you'd really like."

Cole groaned. If it wasn't his mother trying to play matchmaker, it was Dani or Valerie.

"Thanks, but I'm not interested."

Her brows knitted together in a frown. "How are you going to find a mate if you stay at work at all hours of the night and don't go out and meet women?" She lifted her finger before he could respond. "I mean nice women that me and your mother would approve of."

Cole laughed. "I meet plenty of *nice* women on my own, and I'm still not interested in your friend's daughter."

Valerie studied him for a minute, then narrowed her eyes. "Why? Is there someone in your life that you haven't told me about?"

Cole shook his head. "Believe it or not, I don't tell you everything."

"Hmm...I see. Well, I hope that means that you've finally found someone. You're too good of a man to still be walking around single. Let some nice, lucky woman have a shot at you," she said and strolled out of the office.

"I would if the woman I wanted would give me a chance," he mumbled under his breath. Until then, he'd just keep making money for his clients.

CHAPTER THREE

Malaya was still smiling when she walked out of her economics class. The extra day of studying had paid off, and an "A" was her reward. If she kept this up, she'd ace all of her classes this semester.

She adjusted her backpack strap on her shoulder and made her way through the crowded hallway, shimmying around people to get to the exit. Since it was her short day, and economics had been her last class, she couldn't wait to get home and make a nice lunch.

Just as she stepped outside, her cell phone rang. She dug it out of the side pocket of her backpack and assumed it was Dani calling to see if she could work. Instead, Destiny's beautiful face appeared on the screen.

"Destiny?" she said in a rush, surprised her daughter was calling in the middle of a school day. "What's going on? Are you all right?"

"Mommy, can I come to your apartment after school?" she whispered.

Malaya was frowning as she moved out of the flow of foot traffic and found a quiet spot on the side of the building.

"Honey, where are you?"

"I'm in the girl's bathroom. I wanted to talk to you before

recess. Can I come?" she asked in a small voice that pierced Malaya right in the heart. Destiny didn't ask for much, and when she did, Malaya tried to deliver.

"I would love for you to come to my place, sweetie, but it's a school day. I'm not scheduled to see you until next weekend. Did something happen? Why do you want to come today?"

"Daddy and Selena are out of town. I want to stay with you instead of Ms. Becca," she said, referring to the nanny.

Irritation simmered inside of Malaya. She was always willing to have her daughter stay with her. Even if getting her to the other side of town for school would've been challenging, she would've found a way.

"Please, Mommy," Destiny sobbed, and the ragged sound broke Malaya's heart.

"How long is your dad planning to be gone? Do you know?"

"He said a week. I asked if I could stay with you, but he said no." She was outright crying now.

"Honey, don't cry." Malaya had to fight back her own emotions. She hated when her child cried, especially if she wasn't there to console her. "How about if I call him and see if it's okay if I pick you up from home later?"

Malaya could still hear Destiny sniffling on the phone. They both already knew what Todd's answer would be. Which was probably why Destiny didn't respond right away.

"He's just going to say no," her daughter whined, but quieted when a teacher's voice echoed in the background, instructing kids to hurry up and wash their hands.

"I'll try anyway, okay? If he won't let me pick you up and let you stay the week at my place, I'll come and hang out with you for a couple of hours tonight. That could be fun, right?"

There were a few more sniffles before Destiny agreed. After promising that she'd call her later, Malaya disconnected the call. Her heart ached and she blinked back her own tears. She shouldn't have to ask to see her daughter. More than anything, she should always be given the option to take Destiny whenever Todd was out of town.

I can't keep going through this. Something has to give.

She swiped at her eyes and glanced around. At least it had stopped raining and the sun was out, but her happy mood had dried up. The last thing she wanted to do was go home. She had to do something about Todd, and sooner rather than later.

Huffing out a breath, she glanced at her phone. He was the last person she wanted to talk to, especially while she was pissed. Angry words would be exchanged and before she knew it, the situation would be worse.

Maybe she should call Dani first. She was her usual sounding board, but Malaya knew her friend was sick of hearing anything regarding Todd. Dani had even offered to pay to send Malaya and Destiny far away where he couldn't find them.

If only that was an option.

No. Malaya needed another plan, but right now she needed to talk to Todd.

*

Malaya nibbled on her bottom lip as she stood in front of the receptionist desk at Cole's office. She felt so out of place in the luxurious space. Comfortable-looking white leather furniture was strategically placed around the room and expensive art covered the walls. There were several hallways that broke off from the waiting area, making her think the place was even bigger than she first thought.

Maybe showing up unannounced wasn't a good idea.

She had called Todd and the conversation went exactly as she expected. Not only did he ream her out for calling him while on a business trip, but he also told her she couldn't hang out at his house. He didn't want her there while he was out of town.

She could respect that, but she hated the control he had when it came to her spending time with Destiny. Each year, he grew meaner and more unreasonable. It was time to insist on some changes. She just needed to figure out what to do first. Which was how she ended up at Cole's job.

He had told her more than once to come to him if she ever needed assistance. He might've been tossing the offer out there just to be nice, but she didn't think so. Today, she needed his help, or at least his opinion.

The receptionist hung up the phone and glanced at her. "Mr. Eubanks' assistant will be with you shortly. You're welcome to have a seat if you'd like." She pointed to one of the white sofas a few feet away.

"Thank you."

She moved from the desk and set her backpack next to the sofa, but she was too wired to sit. She paced the open area, her footsteps silent against the plush carpet. Maybe she should leave and just call Cole later.

"Hello."

Malaya glanced up at the older woman who was about her mother's age, and like the others in the office, she was professionally dressed. Wearing a stylish, burgundy skirted suit and modest pumps in the same color, the woman sized Malaya up.

"I'm Valerie, Mr. Eubanks' assistant. Do you have an appointment?"

"No, I'm sorry. I don't."

Valerie's gaze traveled up and down Malaya again and her eyes softened. "Is this business or personal?"

"It's personal," Malaya said quietly. "You know what? I shouldn't have come. I'll talk to Cole later. I'm sorry to bother—"

"Just hold on a second." Valerie moved closer to the receptionist desk. "You're here now. Let me see if he's available. Your name again?"

Malaya had given it to the receptionist, but repeated it to Valerie. His assistant picked up the phone and dialed.

"Mr. Eubanks, are you available to meet with Malaya Radcliff? She's in the…" She stopped speaking and listened, then smiled. "Okay. I'll let her know." Valerie handed the phone back to the receptionist and gave Malaya a wide smile. "He'll be right with you. Can I get you something to drink?

Water? Coffee? Juice or maybe a soda?"

"Coffee would be great if it's not too much…" The rest of her words lodged in her throat when Cole appeared from down one of the hallways.

He was a sexy man on any given day, but right now, he was absolutely breathtaking. The dark-blue three-piece suit that molded over his muscular body had him looking like a confident executive ready to close on a seven-figure deal. The light blue dress shirt combined with the paisley tie pulled the whole outfit together perfectly. If she had money to invest, Cole's powerful appearance would have her ready to hand over her cash.

"Hey. You all right?" he asked in a rush as he approached. Concern was etched in his handsome face as he gave her a quick once-over, then slipped his arm around her shoulders. "What's going on?"

Not only did he look good, but he smelled amazing. Whatever fragrance he was wearing—a clean, citrusy scent— was different than he'd worn the other night. Yet it was just as potent and had all of her girlie parts coming to life.

"I'm fine. I'm sorry to just drop by, but—"

"You already know you can stop by anytime. Let's talk in my office." He started ushering her away, but Malaya stopped.

"Are you sure? I don't mind waiting if you're in the middle of something."

"I have time. It'll be a little while before my next appointment."

"Malaya, I'll bring the coffee to the office," Valerie interrupted before walking away.

Malaya grabbed her backpack, and Cole took it from her, slinging it onto his shoulder. His other hand went to the small of her back and a sweet thrill galloped through her body. He'd given her hugs or a quick peck on the cheek on occasion, but this was more intimate. Like he was somehow shielding her from the outside world. Or it could be that her imagination was getting the best of her, and she was reading too much into the moment. That didn't stop her from reveling in his nearness.

"All right, here we are," he said when they reached the last door at the end of the hall. "Come in and make yourself comfortable. Have you eaten today?"

Cole set her backpack in one of the chairs at the small round conference table. He studied her in that way that was a mixture of concern and gentleness. The expression always made her feel special and tingly inside.

"I'll take your silence as a 'no, you haven't.'"

"Oh, sorry. I haven't eaten, but I'll wait until I get home to fix something."

She didn't have to work at the bar later, but she had agreed to do some data entry for a small business who contracted with her on occasion.

"Nonsense. I haven't eaten lunch, so I'll have something delivered for both of us." He pulled out his cell phone. "If I order from one of the restaurants downstairs, food can be delivered within fifteen minutes. Any requests?"

Malaya could've kissed Cole for his thoughtfulness. She was so hungry, even a stale slice of bread would be satisfying. "Anything. Or if there's something you usually order, that'll work." She wasn't picky and as a foodie, she was always game for trying something new.

"You got it."

While he was on the phone, Malaya roamed around his large corner office. She strolled past the stately mahogany desk and made her way to the tall window and gazed out. The firm was located in one of the tallest office buildings in the heart of downtown Atlanta, and they were on the fiftieth floor with a spectacular view.

"Okay, the food will be here shortly. Let's have a seat so you can tell me what's going on."

Before they were seated, a knock sounded at the door and Cole opened it. Valerie strolled in with a silver tray loaded with a coffee carafe, mugs, creamer, and sugar.

"Do you want me to have lunch brought up for you two?" she asked Cole.

"Already taken care of, but thank you."

Once Valerie left, Cole filled their mugs and handed her one, along with two packets of sugar. It was moments like this that reminded Malaya of how well he knew her.

"Talk to me," he said, sitting in the chair next to her and seeming so comfortable in his skin while she was suddenly nervous.

"Destiny called me an hour ago crying, saying that she wanted to live with me."

"Did something happen?"

Malaya recounted that conversation, and told him about her plan to hang out with Destiny later; a plan that got shot down by Todd.

"He told me that I couldn't be in his house or on the premises while he and his wife weren't there. I respect that. All I want is to see my child. I told him that I would rather pick Destiny up and let her stay with me while they were out of town."

"Which makes total sense. What did he say?"

Frustration stirred within Malaya, and she felt so helpless in this situation. "He lost it. Yelling that if I took Destiny, he would get the authorities involve and say that I kidnapped her."

Cole's brows drew together. "Seriously?"

"Cole, I can't keep going through this with him. I hate this setup, and I want my daughter." Her voice cracked on the last word.

Never in a million years did she imagine that she'd be carrying around so much baggage. After Destiny was born, life hadn't been ideal. Yet, each time she looked into her child's beautiful face, their world seemed perfect. At least until Malaya made a mess of everything.

"It's not the first time Destiny has asked to live with me. Now that she's ten, the conversation has been coming up even more, especially when she's left with Todd's wife or the nanny. If only he'd let her stay with me during those times, that would eliminate some of the issues, but when I talked to him Friday night, he didn't mention that he was leaving town."

"Does he usually let you know?"

Malaya shook her head, and a sudden bout of sadness settled in her chest. "Todd doesn't see a reason to tell me anything. He claims I'm not a good mother."

"Well, I know for a fact that you're an amazing mother. What's he basing his opinion on?"

"The past," she said simply, and she only had herself to blame. "We met when I was in college, but we didn't get together until I was twenty-three and had dropped out of school. I've done a lot of growing up over the last few years, but he still sees me as that immature, needy girl I was when we first got married." Malaya met Cole's intense gaze. "I'm not that person anymore, and I want to take him back to court. I'm just trying to put a few things in order."

"A few things like what?"

Malaya's hands were wrapped around the coffee mug as she stared into the dark liquid. She spent eight years with Todd, seven of those as his wife. Three years ago, he kicked her out of his house and divorced her.

Unable to sit still, she stood and paced around the spacious office. "One of the reasons my ex-husband was awarded custody of Destiny is because I didn't have anything after we divorced. No job. No money. No place to live."

"How's that possible? With the divorce, you were entitled to half of everything."

Malaya rubbed her forehead, her mood sinking even lower. "I signed a prenup. I only walked away with my clothes, and I couldn't even keep his last name."

Cole's brows shot up. "Seriously?"

"Yeah. Todd is ten years older than me, and when we met, he was already established. Besides that, he comes from money. I didn't have anything going into our relationship, and I thought our marriage would last." She shrugged. "I was totally dependent on him."

Cole stood in front of her. "That was then. In a few months, you'll have your degree. Then you'll be in a better position to get a full-time job in your field, and everything else will fall into place."

"You make it sound so easy."

"I know it's not, but nothing's impossible."

He pulled her into a hug and Malaya rested her head against him. Being in his comforting, strong arms usually made her forget her problems. This time, though, the heaviness inside her chest didn't loosen. The suffocating sensation was too much.

"Don't let Todd get inside your head. Stay the course and keep working toward your goals."

"I wish I had your confidence. It's taking too long for me to get my act together, Cole. In the meantime, my baby is miserable."

Someone knocked on the office door, but Cole didn't make a move to answer it.

"Go ahead and get that." Malaya started pulling away.

"They can wait."

"No, it's probably lunch, or someone who needs to talk to you. I can wait."

She turned her back and rubbed her chest as if that would help settle the anxiety building inside of her. She was an adult…a grown woman. When would she start feeling like one?

The enticing aroma of basil, oregano, and sage wafted through the air, and Malaya's stomach chose that moment to growl.

"That smells amazing."

"And it's going to taste even better." Cole set the bags on the table. Then he stood in front of her again and grasped both of her hands. "What made you come to me?"

Malaya stared into his light-brown eyes. Her pulse amped up as a potent force traveled between them. The man had such a visceral effect on her, and there were times like now that she could barely think straight.

"That's a good question. I guess…usually, when I'm in your presence, I feel capable, more powerful than I do when I'm alone." That was the truth, even though she hadn't considered that when making the decision to show up at his workplace.

"You are a strong woman. I've watched you for a while now and your fortitude amazes me."

Cole lifted her left hand and brought it to his lips. Without breaking eye contact, he kissed the back of her fingers, and a delicious tingle surged up Malaya's arm and sent heat blasting through her body.

"What can I do for you?" he asked.

If he knew how loaded that question was, he'd probably rephrase it. That sweet kiss and the intensity pulsing between them was thrilling and unnerving at the same time.

What would happen if he kissed other parts of her body? Sure, she'd been attracted to him from day one, but something so electrifying had just passed between them. Malaya would love to take the time to explore the feeling, but right now, she had to stay focused.

"Help me get my daughter back."

CHAPTER FOUR

"Let's eat while we finish talking," Cole said, and gestured for Malaya to reclaim her seat.

As he pulled food containers out of the bag, his mind was going a mile a minute. Seeing the sadness in her eyes moments ago had almost done him in. He wanted to comfort her, hold her close, and promise that everything would be all right.

He also wanted to kiss her—and not just the back of her hand.

What the hell had gotten into him? If he ever wanted a real chance with her, he had to tread lightly. She might've come off as a tough woman, but he hadn't missed the vulnerability he'd just seen in her eyes. Still, that hadn't stopped him from wanting to kiss her enticing lips.

Cole sat in the chair next to her. "Exactly what can I do to help?"

When Valerie informed him that Malaya was there, he had immediately thought the worst, that she or Destiny were hurt or in some type of trouble. He hated she was having problems with Todd, but Cole was glad she had come to him.

She dug into her food as if she hadn't eaten in days. "I don't think there's anything you can do."

Her moans were doing something to him, but Cole couldn't much blame her. The *caponata* was one of his favorite

Sicilian dishes and the first time he'd eaten it, he'd had the same reaction. A medley of vegetables, it contained eggplant, tomatoes, capers, nuts, raisins, and a few additional ingredients that blended perfectly together.

"There's nothing I can do?" he asked. "You want my help, but you don't want me to do anything?"

"Well, maybe not nothing, but I'm not sure. I need to figure out what to do first. I already know I'll have to show that I can support both Destiny and myself, and I'll need to get at least a two-bedroom place. Before any of that can happen, I have to find a full-time job."

"If you need more hours, just—"

"Nope," she said, cutting him off. "Dani offered to give me as many hours as I can handle, but when I go to court to fight for custody, I don't want to have to say I work in a bar."

"I see your point."

"One of my problems is that I started sending out my resumé a few months ago, but no one's interested in hiring me. Until I can find full-time employment, I can't afford a better place to live. And I probably won't be able to find the type of job I need until after I get my degree. It's like a vicious circle."

Cole nodded, totally understanding. All most people needed was a break, and when it came to landing a decent job these days, you almost had to know someone. Lucky for her, he knew a few people who owned their own businesses. It wouldn't take much to put a few feelers out there on her behalf.

"Cole, I didn't come here for you to do anything for me," Malaya said, as if reading his mind. "I mainly came to you to brainstorm ideas, but this is something I have to do myself."

"Why?"

Her brows dipped into a frown. "Why what?"

"Why do you have to do this yourself?"

"Because I don't want to have to depend on anyone. One of the biggest mistakes I made with Todd is that I was too dependent on him."

"I'm not Todd," Cole said with more bite than he intended.

"I know, but I also know me. I've made so many bad choices in the past and… I guess I just don't want to fall back into the habit of depending on others, especially after working so hard to be independent."

She shared a little about her past, telling him about her deeply religious parents who had sheltered her for much of her life. So, when she'd gone off to college with newfound freedom, she didn't know how to act.

"I hooked up with the wrong group of kids and started partying with them practically every night. I wanted to fit in and have some fun for a change. Eventually, my grades dropped which resulted in a few failed classes. I was smart enough to do the work. I just lost focus."

"I take it that didn't go over well with your parents," Cole said already knowing the answer.

"Ha! That's an understatement. In their defense, they gave me plenty of warnings and opportunity to get my act together. But when I didn't straighten up in my sophomore year, they cut me off.

"Needless to say, that put a strain on our already shaky relationship. They said that since I thought I was grown, I could fund my own college. Let's just say that I learned *real* quick that even if you're an adult, you're not grown until you can pay your own way.

"Anyway, I eventually dropped out of school. I didn't want to take out loans. Instead, I found part-time work, thinking that I'd save up and then return to school. You can probably guess how that went."

Cole nodded. He'd gone to college on a partial scholarship. It helped, but had it not been for his parent's assistance, he would've had to work while in school, or end up with a boatload of student loans.

"I mostly sofa-surfed," Malaya continued. "I camped out at some of my friend's places because I couldn't afford my own spot."

The woman she was describing was nothing like the woman Cole had grown to care about. The Malaya he knew was focused, self-reliant, and hard-working. Cole couldn't picture her any other way.

"Man, I kept making one bad decision after another," she continued.

"Like?"

"Like…stuff that would take much longer than an afternoon to share." She gave a nervous laugh and that sadness in her eyes he had witnessed earlier returned.

"Okay, I guess that means you'll have to let me take you out to dinner one day so that you can tell me everything else about yourself."

A slow smile lifted the corners of her lips, and it was like the sun was peeking from behind a cloud.

"Okay," she said.

Cole's brows shot up. "Oookay? Are you finally saying yes to me? Am I hearing you correctly?"

Now she was full-on grinning and her smile lit up the room. Cole wanted to keep her smiling and laughing if she'd let him.

"Yes, I'm saying yes to dinner, and I'll even cook."

"Now you're talking!" She was a great cook. "Let me grab my calendar. I want us to pick a date before you change your mind."

"I won't."

"Okay, good. Tell me about Todd. Why didn't things work out between you two?"

Cole figured the more he knew about the guy and their history, the better they'd be able to come up with next steps. He planned to help Malaya whether she wanted him to or not, but he didn't want to do anything that would make her situation worse.

Malaya picked at the little food that she had left. "I met him when I worked in a print shop that his company used. He'd come in all the time, flirt, and ask me out. At first, I said no, but after a while we started hanging out."

She set the fork down and sighed loudly. "A few months into our relationship, Todd suggested I move in with him. It was perfect timing because I needed a place to stay, and we got along well. He was basically supporting me, and I was doing everything I could to please him. Cooking, cleaning, whatever it took to make him happy. I thought I was in love, and when I found out I was pregnant, he asked me to marry him. That's when things started changing."

"Why? He didn't want the baby?"

"No, nothing like that. We both were excited, but *I* started changing. I wanted more for myself. I was getting ready to be a mother and I wanted my child to be proud of me. I figured once Destiny was old enough, I'd go back and finish my degree. So, I started making my desires known."

"I take it Todd didn't like the idea of you going back to school."

"Nope. He thought that since he was taking care of Destiny and me that I didn't need a college degree. He couldn't understand that I wanted to actually accomplish something with my life. During one of our many arguments, I made it clear that he didn't own me. Big mistake."

"Is that when he made you leave the house?"

Malaya nodded. When Cole saw that she was blinking back tears, he covered her hand with his and squeezed. "Tell me the rest," he said quietly, hating how defeated she appeared.

"He didn't make me leave. He literally dragged me out of the house after I told him I could do whatever I wanted. Considering I didn't have anything, I was talking pretty tough, especially when I told him I'd take Destiny and leave." She pulled her hand from his grasp. "That was three years ago, and you pretty much know the rest."

Cole sat back and ran his hand over his mouth and down his bearded chin. She wasn't as destitute as she'd been back then, but...

"Are you ready to have Destiny full-time? I hear that being a single parent is hard."

Malaya swiped at an errant tear. "I love Destiny more than I love breathing. I didn't think it would take me this long to build a life, but I'll do whatever it takes to have her live with me."

Malaya's words were spoken with such conviction, Cole feared that she'd do something crazy...even something illegal. "All right. I guess we need to form a plan."

CHAPTER FIVE

"Dang, Cole. You almost hit the flagstick. Nice!" Randall Olsten said as he stared openmouthed down the fairway. "'Bout time you started acting like you came to play."

"Whatever, man. You should be glad I'm not out here kicking your butt like usual." Cole returned his driver to his golf bag and tugged on his pushcart.

"Okay, we've been playing for a couple of hours, and you've been playing like crap. What's on your mind?" Randall asked, and Cole chuckled as they trudged down the right side of the fairway.

They had arrived on the course at the crack of dawn, and Cole's mind was everywhere except on his golf game. He couldn't stop thinking about Malaya.

"I invited you out here so that I could pick your brain. I have a friend who has a situation and—"

"*That's* why you've been distracted. I should've known it had to do with a woman."

"I didn't say it was a woman."

"You didn't have to. You're always focused when it comes to golf, except today. So not only is this about a woman, but she must be more than a friend."

"*Anyway,*" Cole said on a laugh.

That was the problem with talking to people who he'd

known for most of his life. They had grown up on the same block and had played peewee football together. No one— except for maybe Dani—knew him better.

During the conversation with Malaya, Cole had mentioned to her that he had a friend, Randall, who was a family law attorney. She'd been glad to hear that but insisted that she wasn't financially ready to hire a lawyer. Cole offered to cover the cost. She quickly shot that idea down, but gave him permission to discuss her situation.

As they walked, Cole filled his buddy in, only giving him pertinent information. For the next few holes, his friend lobbed questions at him. He mainly wanted to know when and how Todd managed to get custody.

It wasn't until they were on the eleventh hole that Randall asked, "Okay, now exactly who is this woman to you?"

"She's…" Cole started to say *friend*, but Malaya was more than a friend. "She's…important to me."

Randall nodded and a slow smile spread across his face. "I see. I figured as much."

They were both silent as he hit his golf ball off the tee and they watched it take a sharp right into some bushes.

"Damn it. I hope it didn't land in the creek."

Cole was pretty sure it had, but didn't say anything. Instead, he focused on his own shot. He brought his arms back and swung, watching as his ball soared through the air and down the center of the fairway. It landed on the edge of the green, putting him in a good position to get par.

"I'm back!" he yelled, and did a fist pump like he'd seen Tiger Woods do on so many occasions.

"Man, I hate you."

Cole laughed and pounded his friend on the shoulder. "Don't hate the player. Hate the game."

Wanting to finish strong, Cole suggested they table the conversation about Malaya until they were done with the round. Instead, they talked about Randall's family. Married with three kids, he always had entertaining stories, especially about his two boys. They were all like family to Cole, and he looked forward to the day that he could discuss his own kids.

Since his birthday a couple of weeks ago, he constantly thought about how old he was getting. It wouldn't be so bad if all aspects of his life were where he wanted them to be.

"So, about Malaya," Randall said, once they'd finished the eighteenth hole and were headed to the parking lot. "It sounds like she already knows what it's going to take to get her daughter. And as many people as you know, I'm sure one of them could hook her up with full-time employment."

"Yeah, I'm planning to put a call into a friend of mine who I used to box with back in the day."

Hamilton Crosby was a managing partner at a personal security firm. The business was growing, and Cole hoped the company was in need of administrative support, which was what Malaya wanted to do.

"That's good, because when she returns to court, she needs to have everything in order. A good job, a decent place for Destiny and her to live, and she's going to have to prove that she can support herself."

Malaya knew all of that, but she and Cole were both hoping that she could do something in the meantime.

"I haven't had any dealings with Todd or the Stapletons," Randall said, referring to Todd's family. "But I do know that they are well-known in the city. The last thing any of them are going to want is a public custody battle. Maybe once she can show that she has her life in order, she could go back to him and—"

"No. She's done talking to him," Cole said adamantly. If he had his way, she'd never ask anything else of Todd, but until Destiny was under her roof, Malaya had to tread lightly.

"Okay, she can take him to court regarding seeing Destiny more often, especially since Todd travels all the time. I'm actually surprised that the courts ruled that she only gets her every other weekend."

Cole didn't say anything. Based on what Malaya had told him, she didn't have anything to fight him with. What type of *man* did that to the mother of his child? Malaya thought that it wasn't just that he didn't want to pay her child support. He wanted to punish her for that time she threatened to walk out on him. She thought it had also been about appearances, which was why he fought to keep Destiny.

"Still, even if she goes that route for right now, she should at least wait until she has a job and a bigger place to live."

"Yeah, I agree," Cole said as they both sat on their car bumpers and changed out of their golf shoes.

If Cole had his way, he'd give Malaya money, a house, or whatever else she needed to get her daughter.

"If…I mean, when Malaya gets situated, would you be willing to take on her case? How do you feel about going up against Stapleton and his legal team?"

"I have no problem with that, when Malaya's ready. From what I hear of the Stapletons, they have more enemies than friends, but money and power go a long way. She needs to be ready."

Cole was going to have to convince her to accept help, especially if it would get her to her goals quicker. She was so afraid of being dependent on someone that she was risking her and her daughter's future. He was surprised she had even come to him in the first place. Then again, like she said, she'd do anything for Destiny. But how far would she go?

Cole glanced at his watch. He needed to get to the office before his one o'clock meeting. Since his day was starting late, he had already planned to work late.

"I'd better get out of here," he said as he loaded his golf clubs into the trunk and slammed it closed. "Thanks for listening. Hopefully, either me or Malaya will be in touch with you soon."

"Sounds good. Just let me know when she's ready to move forward." He gave Cole a one-armed hug. "You know…you can solve a few of her problems before she goes to court."

Cole's brows drew together. "I already told you. She won't take money from me. She wants to do as much of this on her own as she can. It was probably hard for her to even ask me for attorney recommendations." Cole shrugged and pulled open the driver's side door. "There's not much else I can do for her if she doesn't let me."

"You could marry her."

Cole froze, wondering if he'd heard his friend right. He turned to Randall, who had a huge grin on his face.

"Say what?"

"You heard me. Marry her. You said she was important to you, and I know you. That's Cole talk for I'd do anything for this woman…even marry her."

Cole studied him for the longest time, trying to gauge if he was serious. Then he burst out laughing. "Are you kidding me? *Dude*, you know it's not that easy to just up and marry someone. I've heard of marrying people to stay in the country, but to gain custody of a child?" Cole shook his head. "That's a ridiculous idea even for you."

"Is it, though? Is it really a crazy idea?" He lifted his hands up when Cole started to speak. "Hear me out. You care about this woman and her child. More than anything, you're ready to settle down and have a family. I know you want your own kids, but in this case, you'll already have a head start."

"Man, she won't even date me," Cole said, wondering why he was even entertaining this conversation. "Even if I thought she'd say yes…she's never going to go along with…with an arrangement."

"It doesn't have to be an arrangement. I've listened to how you talked about her situation, and this is the first time you've talked about a wom—"

"I've discussed plenty of women with you."

Randall shook his head. "Not like Malaya. You've talked about how hot some of the ladies were and what they do for a living. All superficial crap. The conversation today was…" He glanced up as if trying to think of the right words before returning his attention to Cole. "The way you looked when discussing Malaya reminded me of how I felt before marrying my wife. You're crazy about her."

"That all might be true, but—"

"How well do the two of you get along?" Randall

interrupted.

"We get along great, but—"

"Do you trust her?"

"Of course, but—"

"Is she good with her daughter? Could you see having a family with her?"

"Yeah, but—"

"Does Dani like her?"

Cole chuckled at that one. Everyone who knew his sister knew she was a hard sell. "Yes, she likes her."

"Okay, here's the most important question." He released a long breath and held up his hands as if trying to figure out how to form the question. "Can she cook?"

Cole burst out laughing. "You're a fool. You know that? I thought you were going to ask me how she is in bed or something."

"I thought about it, but…" He shrugged off whatever else he was going to say. "Seriously though. If this situation was different, and we lived in a perfect world, is she someone you could see yourself married to?"

"Without a doubt," Cole said without hesitation. "But how the hell can I convince her to marry me?"

"Seriously? Remember Tabatha Montgomery from high school?" Cole knew where this was going. "How many of us asked her to the homecoming dance during our junior year."

Cole was grinning now. Tabatha had just transferred to the school, and she was one of the prettiest girls Cole had ever seen. Not only that, she was sweet and smart. Every guy in the school had probably asked her out, but she always said no. Until he asked, and she said yes.

"All I'm saying is that if anyone can convince a woman to marry him, it's you."

With that, his friend climbed into his BMW and left Cole standing there, pondering the conversation. Maybe a marriage of convenience could solve both their problems.

Maybe.

A couple of hours later, Cole pulled his Lexus into the

underground parking garage still thinking about Randall's crazy idea.

Marry her.

It had taken Cole almost a year to talk Malaya into going on a date with him, and even that hadn't happened yet. There was no way he could pop the question and have her take him seriously.

He climbed out of the car with his laptop case and strolled across the garage. The tapping of his dress shoes against the concrete echoed through the enclosed space as he mentally thought about the rest of his day. Since he was starting later than usual, he probably wouldn't get out of there until after eight.

Cole approached the glass doors that led from the garage to the building and used his access card to enter. "Hold the elevator." He jogged toward it, catching it before the doors slid closed. "Thanks for holding... Oh, what's up, Jay?" he said, surprised to see one of the investment managers from his office.

"Hey, Cole. I guess I'm not the only one starting late," Vance said. "I can't remember the last time you've strolled in this late."

"Yeah, my first appointment is not until one. I figured I'd take care of some things before coming in."

"Same here. Actually, I have some news. Guess who popped the question last night," Vance said, a sly smile tilting the right corner of his mouth.

Cole almost groaned. Now he was officially the only person in the office who wasn't in a committed relationship, married, or had a couple of kids.

"I hope she said yes," Cole said of Vance's long-time girlfriend, Maria. The way his co-worker was grinning, it was safe to say that she had.

"Not only yes, but a *hell* yes!" he whooped, and Cole couldn't help but laugh.

He really was happy for the guy and would probably be happier if his own social life weren't so dismal at the moment.

"So, who was the hottie visiting you yesterday?" Vance asked. "And don't even bother trying to play dumb or say she was a client. I saw the two of you when you walked her out. The office gossip is buzzing, and you and your lady are the topic of conversation. You've been holding out on us, man."

Cole shook his head. He worked around some of the most intelligent people he knew, but some of them gossiped like they were still in high school.

"You know I like to keep a few things close to my chest. Besides, the office gossip is a little too intense for me."

Grinning, Vance nodded. "True. Seems everyone is always trying to one-up the next person when it comes to our personal lives." He shrugged. "But it's all good. We all just want to see each other happy and not just as it relates to work, but family, too."

Just then the elevator dinged, signaling they'd arrived on the fiftieth floor and not a moment too soon. Cole didn't want any questions about Malaya, his personal life, or anything else for that matter.

"I'll catch you later," he said as they stepped onto their floor. "And congratulations again."

"Thanks, man."

Cole greeted the receptionist as he walked past her and headed to his office. Randall's suggestion was sounding better and better as the day progressed. Now, all Cole had to do was get Malaya to go along with the idea.

This should be interesting.

CHAPTER SIX

Uncertainty crept through Malaya as she patted the dashboard of her old Ford. "Come on, baby. Just hang in there with me a little while longer."

She was on her way to Cole's house and the car kept sputtering as if it was going to shut off. All she needed was a little more time to scrape up some funds. The vehicle had more than paid for itself, and Malaya honestly couldn't ask for more out of it. Still, she hoped it could get her through the next few months. The mechanic promised that, with another thousand dollars, he could get it running halfway decent. That was two months ago.

"Just a little longer," Malaya cooed and followed the GPS instructions through the Dunwoody neighborhood where Cole lived.

A bit of nervousness mixed with excitement warred within her. She was anxious about having dinner with Cole, but excited to spend time with him. Before the other day, Malaya had been adamant about keeping their relationship friendly, but something changed between them that day at his office. She couldn't quite put her finger on what, but there was something different.

Different enough to make her imagine what it would be like if they actually dated.

Since then, she hadn't been able to stop thinking about Cole. Maybe it was because he hadn't judged her. Granted, some of the things she'd been through in the past were due to poor choices, but not everything. Some was just bad luck, especially how horribly things ended with Todd. She hadn't wanted to tell Cole that her ex-husband had physically removed her from their home, a home that she once considered hers. Yet, Cole didn't judge. He only listened. He didn't treat her as if that situation had been her fault. Not like her parents had.

Malaya would never forget their judgment when she landed on their doorstep that night. She hadn't expected them to coddle her, but she had expected at least a little compassion, something she hadn't received. It was probably for the best. Had they showed empathy, she might not have found a job as fast or moved into her own apartment. Instead, she might've stayed with them longer than necessary.

In twenty yards, turn left onto Chamblee Dunwoody Road, the GPS instructed.

Malaya continued following the directions. She and Cole had talked earlier when he called to confirm that they were still on. He'd given her the code to get into the gated subdivision and told her where to find the spare key in case she beat him home. It was nice knowing that he trusted her.

Her lips lifted into a smile as she thought about how much he'd helped her in the past week. He had connected her with a lawyer, and he'd also managed to get her a job interview with a security firm. The dinner she was preparing was originally meant to give them a chance to get to know each other better. Now it was also going to be Malaya's way of thanking him. He'd done more for her in the past few days than some had ever done for her.

Ten minutes later, she pulled up to the front entrance of the subdivision and punched in the code that Cole had given her. Seconds later, the tall wrought-iron gate slid open and she drove in.

After a few turns, Malaya pulled into the driveway where

the two-car garage door was lifted. She was surprised to see Cole standing there with his cell phone to his ear and his laptop bag draped on his shoulder. He pointed to the vacant spot to the right of his Lexus, and Malaya pulled in beside it.

Once she parked and turned off the car, Cole opened the driver side door. "Kevin, I'll call you back in ten minutes," he said into his phone before disconnecting and giving Malaya his attention. "Hey, you. I thought you'd already be here."

"I thought so, too."

Malaya accepted the hand Cole offered, and an intense tingle scurried up her arm when he helped her out of the car. Would she ever get used to this man's touch? Probably not. She hadn't been touched by any man in years and with Cole, her senses were always on high alert.

"Did you get lost?"

"No, I had to stop at more than one store to get everything I needed."

Cole nodded, and his appreciative gaze slid down her body. "You look nice."

Heat spread to Malaya's cheeks, and with her fair complexion, there was no doubt that he noticed. She'd never been very good at accepting compliments, and he gave them often.

"Thank you."

Along with her usual silver jewelry, she had opted for a soft pink low-cut blouse and black jeans with a pair of ankle boots. The whole outfit had been a generous Christmas gift from Dani. The ensemble wasn't overly dressy, but it was a step up from casual and perfect for a first date.

Well, an *unofficial* first date.

"Here, let me help you with the groceries." Cole opened the rear car door. "Your ride sounded like it was ready to quit."

"I know. This thing has been acting up for the last few days."

"Didn't you just have work done on it?"

"I did." As they carried the groceries into the house, Malaya told him all that the mechanic said was wrong with the car.

They entered the townhouse on the ground level and strolled past a bedroom that had an attached bathroom. Then they climbed the stairs to the main floor where the living room, dining room, kitchen, and a sun room were located. This was Malaya's second time at his place. The first was months ago when he'd had a birthday party for Dani.

As she followed him into the kitchen, Malaya fell in love with Cole's home all over again.

"It's probably time to retire your car," he said. "We should look into getting you a new—"

"There you go with that *we* thing again. Cole, you've done so much for me. There's no way I'm asking anything else of you."

"But you didn't ask," he said, humor glimmering in his gorgeous brown eyes.

"Okay, maybe I didn't, but *I'll* get a car as soon as I can. Until then, I'll make do."

"All right, I'll drop the subject for now. But don't be surprised when I bring it up again."

They set the grocery bags on the long center island, and Cole went back for two more. From her position in the kitchen, Malaya glanced around. The townhouse had a modern design with a black and gray color palette and splashes of bluish gray. They were colors she wouldn't have thought to put together, but they blended beautifully.

She strolled into the living room and ambled over to the fireplace mantle where there were several photographs. The family pictures brought a smile to her face. She and her parents were no longer close, but Cole's family—which consisted of him, Dani, and their parents—looked so happy.

Another framed photo caught Malaya's attention, and she picked it up to get a better look. The shot was of Cole, back in his boxing days. Her pulse amped up as her gaze crept over his wide bare chest and thick, muscular arms, but his six-pack abs had her practically drooling. He had boxed semi-professionally during his last years of college, and from what she'd heard, he could've gone pro. Cole wasn't currently training the way he used to, but he appeared just as fit now.

She continued studying the picture. *Machine-Gun Cole* was printed across the bottom of the photo. Dani had told her that Cole rarely discussed those days. It had something to do with his last fight that had landed his opponent in intensive care. Maybe one day she'd get him to talk about it.

Malaya returned the photo to the mantle. She glanced around at some of the art on the walls before heading back to the kitchen. Top-of-the-line stainless appliances, quartz countertops, and gorgeous hardwood floors stood out from the steel-blue walls. There were more cabinets than she'd ever be able to fill and a pantry that was larger than the kitchen at her apartment.

"That's it," he said, setting the rest of the grocery items on the counter.

"Thanks for bringing everything in. I know I've said this before, but you have a beautiful home."

"Thanks. I'm glad you like it. Make yourself at home." Cole glanced at the platinum watch on his wrist. "I need to finish up that call, but holler if you need anything."

"I'll be fine if you don't mind me going through your cabinets."

"Like I said, make yourself at home. I should be done in about twenty minutes or so."

"Take your time," Malaya said as he jogged up the stairs.

Grabbing her cell phone from her purse, she pulled up her play list and Glenn Jones' voice filled the kitchen. She hummed along and rocked to "Show Me" as she chopped onions, carrots, and celery for her sauce. Malaya was always happiest when she was cooking, especially when she was cooking for someone else. It had been so long since she'd spent one-on-one time with a man, and she was glad it was Cole.

The aroma of braised chicken and homemade scalloped potatoes filled the air. She planned to do asparagus for herself and corn for Cole, who didn't like green vegetables. She'd found that out shortly after she started working at the bar.

Thirty minutes later, Cole strolled into the kitchen. "Mmmm, something smells good. Do you need a taste tester?" he asked, his voice deeper than normal as he stood by her side.

His gaze burned into her, and Malaya swallowed. His body heat and the alluring scent of his cologne was doing wicked things to her peace of mind, let alone the rest of her body.

Tonight, something was different. Cole seemed broader. Taller. And even *finer* than usual. Yet, he was his typical laidback self.

It has to be me.

She hadn't had sex in…hell, she couldn't even remember the last time, and being in Cole's presence wasn't helping. She was so horny that if he wasn't careful, she might jump his fine ass and kiss him senseless.

Malaya shook her head and glanced away. She had to stop her mind from traveling into dangerous territory, and thinking about sex with Cole was definitely dangerous. They were friends, and technically Cole was her boss. She might not report to him, but still… She couldn't afford to screw up their relationship by being reckless. No, she had to be strong and tamp down the sexual tension brewing inside of her.

Malaya cleared her throat and pushed away the sudden desire to kiss his full, tempting lips.

"Um…how—how would you like to taste this red wine sauce that I have for the braised chicken?"

"You don't even have to ask."

Malaya dipped the wood spoon into the pot. When she pulled it out, she placed her other hand beneath it to catch any drips.

"It might be a little hot," she warned.

Cole opened his mouth and at first took a tentative taste before opening wider to take in all of the sauce. His eyes nailed her in place, and Malaya struggled to keep from fidgeting under his penetrating gaze.

"That's delicious. I can't wait to eat," he crooned. The deep tone of his voice settled around her like an intimate embrace, and Malaya wanted to keep him talking. Better yet, she wanted him to stop talking and kiss her long and hard.

Stop it. Stop it. Stop it, her mind screamed.

"Uhh…" she said, flustered.

This was ridiculous. She needed to get a grip and quit acting like a lovestruck high-schooler.

She quickly turned away and dropped the spoon in the sink. "It's going to be a little while longer before dinner is ready. How about if you pour the wine, and I'll finish slicing some apples to go with this cheese?"

Cole pulled two large wine glasses out of the cabinet and grabbed the bottle of Moscato from the refrigerator. "I've had cheese and crackers, but I can't say that I've ever had cheese with apples."

"You've been missing out, then." She took one of the small slices of Havarti cheese that she had cut earlier and added it to the sliced apple. "Here, try this. Open up." She fed Cole the snack and the way he stared into her eyes sent heat that was hotter than fire spreading through her body.

What was she thinking? She hadn't planned to hand-feed him, but it seemed like the most natural thing to do at the moment.

"Wow, that is good. I never would've put those items together."

"I'm glad you like it. Stick with me, and I'll teach you some things."

Cole leaned his hip against the counter and grinned. "I'd love for you to teach me everything you know. Actually, there's something I want to talk to you about."

Malaya glanced at him while she finished slicing another apple, then slid the snack in front of him. "Sounds serious. Is it about Destiny or the lawyer?"

"Sort of. Let's wait until the food is done and we can discuss it over dinner."

Malaya lit the large candle that was in the center of the glass dining table and set out the plates and utensils. "Okay, but I'm not the most patient person. Is it something bad? If it is, let's talk about it now."

"It's nothing bad. Just an idea that I want to run by you."

"Oh, all right."

Once the chicken was done, they carried the serving dishes to the table. She hadn't initially set out to create a romantic atmosphere, but everything together did just that. The table looked amazing.

"How about a toast?" Cole said, once they were seated. He lifted his glass, and Malaya followed suit. "To more than a friendship and a bright future."

A smile eased across her lips. "I'll drink to that."

They were silent when they first dug into their meal, and she was happy with how everything turned out.

"Damn, girl. You know you can cook," Cole said after a few bites.

"Thank you. It's nice to have someone to cook for."

"Well, you can cook for me anytime. So, how was your day?" he asked.

Malaya was so used to eating alone or with Destiny, she couldn't remember the last time she had actually discussed her day. The exception being the conversation and lunch that she and Cole had shared in his office.

"It was good. I had three classes and no exams. That always makes for a good day. Then before I came over here, I helped my neighbor, Mrs. Patterson, with her bills and made a couple of doctor's appointments for her."

"You haven't mentioned her in a while. I didn't realize you were still helping her out."

Mable Patterson was the sweet old lady who lived in the apartment across the hall from Malaya. They'd met when she had first moved in, and Malaya tried helping her as often as possible, especially since she was a widow and her two kids lived in Philadelphia. Her daughter wanted her to move up north to be closer to them, but Mrs. Patterson wasn't interested in moving to the cold.

"What about you? How was your day?"

Cole chuckled. "I can't remember the last time a woman asked me about my day. Or anyone, for that matter. But to answer your question, my day was great because I was looking forward to spending my evening with you." He glanced around the table as if seeing it for the first time. "This is nice. An excellent meal. Great atmosphere. Wonderful company. A guy could get used to this."

"Yeah, me too. This is one of the nicest evenings I've had in a long time."

Cole nodded and lifted his glass of wine to his lips. He peered over the rim at her as he sipped, then set it back on the table.

"Where do you see yourself in five years?" he asked.

"Where do I see myself in five years?" Malaya repeated as she pondered the question. "I'll be thirty-nine then. Of course, I want Destiny living with me, and I'd like to have my degree, as well as a great paying job. But I'd also like to be remarried with one or two more children. I don't know how realistic that is, but if I had my way, that would be my reality."

"Well, I'm a true believer that anything is possible."

"What about you?" Malaya asked. "You've achieved so much already. What else would you like to accomplish in the next five years?"

"That's a good question. I'm proud of what I've accomplished in my professional life, but my personal life needs work."

"I guess working long hours probably puts a dent in your dating life."

"Somewhat, but I work long hours by choice. I love what I do, and since I don't have anyone to come home to..." he shrugged, "I stay at the office."

"I can understand that. I hope to one day have a job that I love, but I guess it probably wouldn't be easy juggling a career and a family."

"No, it won't be easy, but like I said, anything is possible." Cole went back to eating. "Like you, I'm hoping by then I'll be married with at least two or three kids. Actually, I'd like to have a total of four, but that might be pushing it in that time frame."

Malaya smiled at him, thinking that he'd be an irresistible

husband. He already had some of the characteristics that she'd look for in one. Trustworthy. Dependable. Protective. Kind, and he had a great sense of humor. Dani often picked on him, calling him stingy and self-centered at times, but that wasn't how Malaya saw him. At least, that wasn't how he was with her.

Cole was the most giving man she'd ever known. Considering she really only had Todd to compare him to wasn't saying much. Her ex-husband might've provided a roof over her head and clothes on her back, but that's where his generosity had stopped. Anything else he did for her came with strings attached.

Though she missed living in the same house as her daughter, she didn't miss Todd at all. If anything, it was a relief to not be under his thumb. Except part of her still was, since he had Destiny.

Don't go there, she berated herself. She and Cole were having a nice, relaxing evening, and Malaya didn't want to ruin it by thinking about her problems. As they continued eating, she stole glances at him between bites.

Since meeting Cole, she'd always thought that he was out of her league, even though he kept asking her out. What would it be like to date someone like him? Or to date him? Probably fun and exciting if her experience so far with him was any indication.

"What are you smiling about?" he asked, catching her staring at him.

Heat rushed to her cheeks. "I didn't realize I was smiling. I was just thinking…" Her words trailed off and she brought the glass of wine to her lips. No need to share every single thought and reveal how attracted she was to him.

"Thinking about what?" Cole asked and added more scalloped potatoes onto his plate.

Malaya released a nervous laugh. Of course he would ask. "Nothing much. Just…thinking. Anyway, enough about me. What did you want to talk about?"

"Two things, actually."

"What are they?"

"One: Will you be my date for a housewarming party on Sunday?"

Malaya frowned. "People still have those?"

"Apparently so. It's for one of the women from work; she and her husband had a house built and recently moved in. I was planning to just buy a gift and give it to her at work, but my assistant said I need to show up."

"Why?"

"Yeah, that was my question, too." He sighed and stared down at his plate, pushing some of his food around with his fork. "We work in a family-like environment. There's always some celebration going on. Valerie claims I've been finding an excuse not to attend most of these events, especially lately. Anyway, I figured I'd only attend if you go with me," he said, eyeing her in that intense way that he often did.

"Considering all that you've done for me, that's the least I can do. Sure, I'll be your date."

Malaya couldn't stop the grin from spreading across her face. She probably looked silly getting excited about being his date for the party, but she didn't care. She loved hanging out with him.

"Okay, and what's the other thing you wanted to talk about?" she said, stuffing a piece of chicken into her mouth.

"Oh, I was wondering if you'd marry me."

CHAPTER SEVEN

Oh, damn.

Fear gripped Cole and he lunged from his chair. He hurried to the other side of the table where Malaya was suddenly red-faced with her eyes bulging. Her hands gripped her throat as she gasped for air.

"Are you choking?" Cole asked, but knew the answer before she gave a jerky nod and tears filled her eyes.

He pulled her from the chair and stood behind her with his arms wrapped around her waist. He fisted one hand and covered it with the other, trying not to hurt her as he did several quick abdominal thrusts, practically lifting her off the floor with each one. It took six tries before the food flew from her mouth.

Malaya coughed a couple of times, her hand on her chest, before she slumped against him.

"I am so sorry," Cole hurried to say, thinking he could've picked a different way and better time to mention marriage. "Are you okay?"

Malaya nodded, the back of her head brushing against his chest. He tightened his hold around her, and placed a kiss against her temple as his own heart rate slowly went back to normal.

They stood that way for a few minutes before she patted

his hand that was resting against her stomach. "I'm okay," she rasped, still trying to catch her breath.

Cole reluctantly released her, but didn't move away as she reclaimed her seat.

"Are you sure?" He watched her critically as she swiped at her eyes and took in a couple of breaths. "Do you need anything?"

"No, but.... Thank you."

Cole didn't miss the weariness in her eyes. He wasn't sure if it was because of the choking or if the expression had more to do with him asking her to marry him.

"You saved my life," she said quietly and rubbed the front of her neck.

Cole pulled out the chair next to her and dropped down in it. "Are you sure you're all right? I didn't hurt you, did I?" He'd been so keen on clearing her air passage that he didn't think about how much pressure he was using.

"No. I'm not hurt. Just shocked."

"By what just happened or what I said?" he asked and sat back in the seat.

"Maybe both, but I'll admit that your request caught me totally off guard."

"Yeah, sorry about that. I probably should've popped the question when you weren't eating."

Her mouth dropped open. "Wait. You can't be serious about...about...you know."

"Marrying you?"

She nodded.

"I'm dead serious. If you marry me, you'll be one step closer to gaining custody of your daughter."

"By marrying you?" she shrieked, and lurched out of her seat. "Cole, I appreciate what you've done for me, but marriage? That's crazy!"

"Is it? People get married for all types of reasons." Now he sounded like Randall, but Cole had totally embraced the idea since that morning at the golf course. "I don't think it's crazy at all."

"Then we need to get your head examined."

He laughed and grabbed his half-empty plate and resumed eating while she paced, something she did often when thinking. Malaya stopped near the table and jammed her hands onto her hips. "How can you eat during a time like this?"

Cole's fork stopped just short of his mouth, and he stared at her with raised brows. "A time like what?"

"A time when you just asked me to marry you. How can you eat when you're thinking about throwing away your whole life...for me?"

"Whoa, baby."

Cole set his fork down and wiped his mouth before standing. With his hands on her shoulders, he forced her to look at him.

"First of all, marrying you wouldn't be a hardship. Far from it. Second, if you took a moment to think about it, you'll see that it's not a bad idea."

She folded her arms across her chest, forcing him to drop his hands. "Explain."

"Explain what? Why I'd love to marry you?"

"Yes. We haven't even gone on a date. You don't know if we'd even get along—even if it would be a pretend marriage."

"It won't be pretend. When I...when *we* say *I do*, it will be for real. I'm not proposing some fake marriage. This will all be real."

Malaya threw up her hands and started pacing again. "Now you're really talking crazy. We haven't even kissed."

Taking that as a challenge, Cole stuck out his arm and caught her around the waist and pulled her to him. He cupped her face between his hands, and before she could protest, he lowered his mouth to hers.

For months, he had wanted to taste her sweetness, and finally he was getting the chance. When her lips parted, giving him full access to her soft, velvety mouth, he knew one kiss would never be enough. Their tongues tangled, swirling around each other as if this wasn't the first time. The drugging kiss exceeded anything he could've imagined and had his senses reeling, and his mind short-circuiting.

Man, this woman.

When he'd decided to pose the idea, Cole hadn't planned to kiss her. At least not yet. Not until she agreed to his proposition. But damned if he wasn't glad the conversation veered in this direction.

Cole slid his hand behind her head and held her close while increasing their connection. His pulse pounded, and desire roared through his body, stirring a passion he hadn't felt in a long time. This was what he wanted. She was who he wanted in his life going forward.

When the kiss finally ended, Cole slowly lifted his head but he didn't release her. They were both panting as if they'd sprinted a mile around a track, and yet, he wanted more. The dreamy expression in Malaya's eyes and her kiss-swollen lips made him want to taste her all over again.

So, he did.

Malaya wrapped her arms around his neck and her fingers sifted through the back of his hair. Her touch had heat seeping into his scalp and spreading through his body like a roaring wildfire. A moan pierced the air, and Cole's arms went around her small waist, bringing her flush against his body. She fit so perfectly in his arms and the feel of her womanly curves molded against his frame was doing wicked things to him.

The first kiss had been exploratory, feeding Cole's curiosity. But this? This one was hot and demanding, and the longer it lasted confirmed what he already knew; they would be amazing together.

Malaya moaned, or maybe it was him. It didn't matter. The burning desire roaring through his body had him wanting more, but he had to tamp down the sudden need to carry her up to his bedroom. The last thing he wanted to do was move any faster and scare her away.

This time when the kiss ended, Cole slowly dropped his arms from around her and took a step back. "That's just one proof that my idea is a good one."

Malaya touched her fingers to her mouth tentatively as she

watched him. "Wow. That was…wow," she said breathlessly. "I—I—I can't believe you just…we just… Aww, hell. You got me all flustered."

Then I've done my job, Cole wanted to say, but kept the thought to himself.

"I can't believe we're even having this conversation." She released a nervous laugh and ran her fingers through her kinky afro before shaking her head. "I can't mar—"

"Don't say no," he interrupted. "Not yet. Not before you think seriously about what I'm proposing."

"Cole, this is not one of your million-dollar deals that you're putting together for a client. This is our life…*your* life. What happens when your soul mate comes along and you want to marry her? I'd do anything to get Destiny, but I don't want to go through a divorce again. I don't want to put her through something like that. Heck, I hope you never have to experience anything like that."

"Divorce is not an option. If we get married…*when* we get married, we stay married. We can hammer out all the details, make sure we are clear on every aspect of our union, but divorce? Never gonna happen."

His parents had married shortly after meeting each other and had been married for forty-five years. Cole had no doubt that what he was proposing could work. His parents had professed their love to each other before getting married, but they'd learned quickly that marriage took way more than just love.

Malaya released a humorless laugh and grabbed the sides of her head as if in pain. "This is insane! I can't marry you, Cole. We're not in love."

Cole pulled her into his arms and lifted her chin with the pad of his finger, forcing her to look at him. "I love you."

She swatted his chest. "You know what I mean. I love you, too, but I'm talking about a romantic love. The type of love people experienced when—when…when they're in love and ready to marry someone."

"Were you in love with Todd when you married him?"

Malaya's brows drew together slightly, and she lowered her gaze. As she stared at his chest, she bit down on her bottom lip.

"Were you?" Cole repeated.

"I thought I was, but I'm not sure."

"Like I said before, people get married for all types of reasons. Sure, this might sound like a marriage of convenience, but it—"

"It doesn't just sound like it. That's exactly what it would be."

"But it can work. You'll get Destiny. We'll grow as a family, and we'll live happily ever after."

She stared at him for the longest time and rested her hands on his chest. "You make it sound so simple, but we both know that it's not. This is an amazing offer you're making me, and I'd be a fool to turn it down. But Cole, this would be a win-win for *me*. What about you? What do you get out of all of this?"

"What do *I* get?" He cupped her face and stared into her eyes as he brushed his thumb across her soft cheek. "I get you."

CHAPTER EIGHT

"Wait! What do you mean, Cole asked you to marry him?" Dani's voice was a high shriek as she stared at Malaya with wide eyes.

"Not so loud," she shushed and glanced around the boutique's dressing room to see if anyone heard her. Then Malaya took the clothes from Dani's hands and hurried into one of the rooms.

She was glad her friend had agreed to go shopping with her. The few clothes in her closet really weren't ideal for interviewing, especially at a place like Supreme Security. They were a high-end personal security agency, and based on Malaya's research, they hired the best of the best security specialists. She was sure that was the case for all personnel, especially since the company catered to an elite clientele.

Malaya hung the black suit, as well as the brown one, on a hook in the dressing room. She hated shopping. Not just because she rarely had extra money, but also making quick decisions wasn't one of her strengths.

"You need to start talking 'cause I want details," Dani said from the other side of the dressing room door. "When did this happen, and why are you just mentioning this? We've been together for the last twenty minutes. You could have told me on the drive here."

"I assumed you knew, but can we discuss this after we leave? I don't want everyone knowing my business."

"We're the only ones in here. Now start talking."

Malaya gave her the CliffsNotes version, and she also told her about the housewarming party. She promised to tell her the whole story once they were back in the car.

Even then, there would be some parts Malaya would keep to herself. Like that breath-stealing kiss. Actually, it was *kisses*. The second one was even hotter than the first, and their immediate connection blew Malaya's mind.

Sure, she had always been attracted to Cole and had imagined them being together. But those were fantasies. Never in a million years did she think she'd actually get to experience kissing him.

Her pulse amped up, and she fanned herself just thinking about the intense lip-lock. The evening with Cole wouldn't be one she'd soon forget. It had been one shock after another.

Marry me.

It was still hard for her to wrap her brain around that idea. Cole said those two words as if he was asking her to the movies. As if marrying one of your friends wasn't a big deal. As if lives weren't drastically changed when two people commit their lives together...*forever.*

To say she'd been shocked would've been an understatement. She loved him for being willing to sacrifice his freedom, his bachelorhood, and ultimately life as he knew it, for her. She could admit that marrying someone like Cole, a sweetheart of a man who made her body sizzle, wouldn't be much of a hardship.

All night, while tossing and turning in bed, she had weighed the pros and cons of the proposal. There were definitely more pros, especially for her, but what about him? She wasn't buying that all he wanted was her. There had to be something else in it for him, but she couldn't see it. All she could think about at the moment was how she'd benefit in more ways than one.

And that darn kiss.

Their chemistry was definitely throwing a wrench in the idea of her saying—no. There were moments throughout the day that felt as if she could still feel Cole's luscious lips against hers. Which was just crazy. Even married to Todd, she had never been kissed so thoroughly.

Would every aspect of a relationship with Cole be like that? Where she'd be satisfied in every way? That alone almost had Malaya saying yes to his ridiculous idea because she wanted to see what it would be like to be Cole's wife. Actually, the reckless, adventurous side of her wanted to say *'Hell, yeah I'll marry you!'*

What woman in her right mind wouldn't? The man was…everything.

Gorgeous.

Smart.

Financially secure.

He treated her like she was a precious gift.

Oh, and she definitely couldn't forget to add *amazing kisser* to the list.

"I can't believe that jerk popped the question and didn't tell me first," Dani said.

So caught up in her thoughts, Malaya had temporarily forgotten that her friend was on the other side of the door.

"Yeah, I'm surprised, too. I thought he told you everything."

"Apparently, not. So, what did you say when he—" She stopped speaking, and Malaya heard a couple of other women talking animatedly as they entered the dressing room area. "Okay, Laya, besides the suits, you're going to need a cute outfit for the party. I'll be right ba—"

"Stop!" Malaya hurried to say. "I can only buy one of these suits. I'll have to wear something I already have to the party."

"What you have in your closet won't work for that saditty group. Finish trying on the suits. I'll be back."

Someone in the area giggled, and Malaya rolled her eyes. Normally, she was a private person, but with Dani around, it was hard to keep her business to herself.

"Dani," she ground out. When she didn't respond, Malaya glanced under the door and didn't see her friend's feet.

I'm not buying anything else, she thought to herself.

She barely had enough money to cover one of the suits. There was no way she'd be able to afford another outfit, but trying to tell Dani that would be fruitless. The woman did whatever she wanted, rarely caring what others thought.

Malaya stared at herself in the full mirror, admiring how nicely the brown suit fit. The boutique wasn't one she'd normally shop at, but Dani had insisted. She claimed that Malaya should have at least one nice suit in her closet.

She buttoned the double-breasted jacket and ran her hands down the side of the fitted garment. Not only did the material feel amazing against her skin, it also hugged her curves perfectly.

"Open the door and let me see what you look like," Dani said.

"What do you think?" Malaya asked when she opened the door. Imitating a fashion model, she twisted and turned several times in front of her friend. "Well?"

"That looks like it was made for you. How was the black one?"

"It was all right, but the jacket was a little big. I'd have to have it tailored and I don't have time." It was Saturday, and her interview was Wednesday afternoon. "I definitely like this one better."

"Do you have a camisole to wear underneath it, or should I find one here?"

"I have one." Malaya eyed the clothing items in Dani's hands. "I'm not buying all of that."

Dani shoved the clothes at her. "Try them on."

"Dani, I can't—"

"Try. Them. On," she demanded and slammed the door closed.

"Well, alrighty then," Malaya mumbled. She tried the flirty red dress on first, loving how the satiny material slid over her body and stopped just above her knees.

"Whoa," she breathed and slid her hands over the soft fabric. She turned and glanced over her shoulder at the numerous straps that crisscrossed in the back and stopped just above her butt.

The outfit wasn't really her style, but she loved everything about the design. Malaya didn't dare look at the price. No doubt it was out of her price range, but she'd be lying if she said that she didn't love the way the dress flowed over her body.

"Let me see whatever you have on," Dani instructed.

"All right." She opened the door, and Dani's jaw dropped. It wasn't often her friend was caught speechless.

"Oh, we are definitely getting that one. Girrrl, my brother is going to swallow his tongue when—"

"I already told you that I can't—"

"Your future husband is covering this little shopping spree," Dani said, a huge Cheshire grin spread across her face. "I just talked to him. There's no budget. Now hurry up and try on the other two outfits."

Now Malaya was the one standing with her mouth hanging open. "But I didn't give him an answer."

Despite his compelling argument, Malaya never agreed to his proposition.

Or should she be referring to it as a proposal? She wasn't sure.

Either way, the idea seemed too crazy for her to consider saying yes. For most of the conversation she'd found it hard to take him seriously. That was, until she'd asked him what he'd get out of the arrangement.

I get you, he'd said, and totally rocked her from the inside out. The scary part was that he was dead serious.

Malaya started to tell Dani that there was no way she could accept such an expensive gift from Cole, but Dani lifted her hand before she could get a word out.

"The sooner you try on the outfits, the sooner we can get out of here. Now, hurry up."

"I can't let him pa—"

"Dang, Laya. Just once, can you let someone do

something nice for you?" Exasperation dripped from each word.

Didn't she realize that they were always doing nice things for her? The biggest thing was giving her a job when she needed it most.

"Don't you want to look nice for the party?"

"Yeah, but—"

"No buts, try on the damn clothes."

Malaya huffed out a breath. "Fine."

She'd try on the clothes, but she wasn't letting Cole or Dani pay for anything. She had worked too hard to gain her independence.

The last thing she planned to do was allow another man to come along and pay for everything for her. That's how things started with Todd, and she refused to go that route with Cole. She couldn't go down that road again.

That's why I can't marry him, she told herself. She had entertained the idea throughout the night, but now she knew for sure that she couldn't accept that type of help from him.

Once she got the job at Supreme, she would save every penny. It might take a few months to get a new place, but she'd do it. And she would do it on her own terms.

I just hope it doesn't take forever.

*

Cole's breaths came in short spurts as he threw punches in rapid succession, trying to free his mind of Malaya. It was no use. Every other thought was of her, and the more he recalled of the conversation they'd had an hour ago, the more frustrated he got.

He threw a right hook, followed by an uppercut catching Braxton on the chin. His friend then came back with a solid punch to Cole's ribs, meaning Cole needed to stay alert and keep his head in the match. Braxton was holding his own, and it didn't matter that Cole put more power behind each punch.

This was what he needed. Sparring at a boxing gym usually helped him work out his problems and right now, Malaya was a problem. She'd said no to his proposal. It didn't matter that it would help her get closer to reaching her goals. She thought marrying her would keep him from finding his soul mate. He didn't know how to make her see that they were perfect for each other. They might not have that I-can't-live-without-you love, but they had something better. A solid friendship and a chemistry that most married people would kill for.

Cole threw harder punches.

Jab-cross-left uppercut-cross.

Jab-cross-hook-cross.

He mixed up his combination and appreciated that Braxton was hanging in there. This was their third round of going for two-and-a-half minutes and they'd been going hard. Sweat dripped from every pore of Cole's body, and he could go longer, but it wouldn't be safe. It had been a while since he'd climbed into a ring, and the last thing either of them needed was an injury.

He blocked Braxton's next couple of jabs, but missed one, taking a punch to his chest and another near his shoulder. Cole adjusted his footwork, shuffled left and right, and landed several shots that caught his friend off guard.

Boxing semi-professionally during college, Cole had rose up the ranks pretty quickly. According to his trainer at the time, he could've gone pro. He had actually considered it until his last fight. He had knocked out competitors in the past, but that night he'd had to watch one of them get carted off on a stretcher. Knowing he could've killed the man had shaken Cole to the point of him never stepping into the ring professionally. But it hadn't stopped him from boxing recreationally.

He and Braxton kept moving around the ring as the sound of other boxers grunting, yelling, and gloves hitting gloves added to the energized hum of the gym. A hum that used to fuel Cole back in the day and still invigorated him.

He threw a punch with his left, followed by another uppercut with his right. Braxton was good, but Cole noticed how he kept dropping his left hand, giving Cole too many opportunities to connect with the left side of his face. They might've been wearing headgear, but it was still a weakness that could cause some painful blows.

A minute later, they stopped and bumped gloves. There were two high-schoolers outside of the ropes who helped them with their gear.

"Machine-Gun Cole," Terrance, a man Cole had sparred with a few times in the past, said as he approached them. "I haven't seen you around in a while. Where you been?"

Cole removed his mouthpiece. "What's up, man. Yeah, it has been a while. Looks like you're still working out often." He was definitely more cut and fit than Cole remembered.

The man grinned. "You know how it is. Just trying to be like you."

Cole introduced him to Braxton, and they talked for a few minutes before Cole and Braxton excused themselves.

"Damn. You were like a madman in that ring," Braxton said on a laugh as they headed to the hallway that would take them to the locker room. "Next time I'll have to gauge your mood before stepping in there with you."

"Too much for you, huh?"

"Nah, bro. You know I can handle anything you throw my way, but I'll admit, you worked me today. Between boxing with you, and later hanging with Debra's rug rats," he said, referring to his sister's kids, "It's going to take me all day tomorrow to recover before heading into work Monday."

"Let me guess. You guys have another huge project," Cole said.

A computer network architect, Braxton worked for Computer Systems Design company, one of the largest tech companies in Atlanta. They always seemed to be working on one major project after another.

"You know it, and I probably shouldn't have been in that ring with you. Feels like I'm all bruised up."

"It doesn't even look like I touched you. I can tell you've been practicing. You still need to remember to keep that left hand up. You were dropping it to your side."

Braxton nodded. "Thanks. I hadn't realized it until your glove kept making contact with my jaw."

They both laughed and discussed their sparring match as they made their way down the hallway that would lead to the locker room.

"So, what's going on with you?" Braxton asked. "It was as if you were fighting off some demons out there."

"I asked Malaya to marry me."

Braxton's brows dipped into a frown and he stopped in his tracks. "Say what now? You actually proposed to her? Hell, I didn't even know you two were dating. You've been holding out."

They stepped off to the side and Cole shared some of what had been going on with Malaya. Braxton, like Axel, was like a brother to him, and he knew he could trust them both with anything.

"She called me right before I arrived here and said thanks, but no thanks."

Just discussing the proposal with his friend frustrated Cole all over again. Even though she hadn't been able to stop thanking him for the offer, telling him how flattered she was, she wouldn't budge. She didn't want to get married just to improve her chances of custody. She said the next time she married, she wanted it to be for love.

Cole had known the idea would be a hard sell. But considering what she had to gain, he thought she'd say yes. Not only that, he and Malaya had been skirting around each other since she'd been hired at the bar. The attraction was getting harder to ignore, and Cole knew she was feeling it, too.

It also bugged the hell out of him that Malaya had refused to let him pay for her purchases during her shopping trip earlier. It wasn't just that. He couldn't figure out why she was so against someone helping her. Yes, he could understand her wanting to stand on her own, but everyone needed a helping hand on occasion.

"Well, at least she finally agreed to go out with you. That's progress."

True, but Cole wanted more. After Dani had finished shopping with Malaya, she had called Cole. She might've been all for his reason for proposing, but she still insisted that he was mainly doing it for selfish reasons.

If he was honest with himself, he knew a big part of wanting to marry Malaya was because he was ready to have a family. She was everything he wanted in a wife, and he didn't see anything wrong with going after her.

Was he madly and passionately in love with her? Maybe not, but he cared more about her than he'd ever cared for another woman. Sure, their union might start as a marriage of convenience, but he could see himself easily falling in love with her.

"Well, I'm the last person who should be giving advice. I have my own challenges with Londyn," he said of the woman he was currently dating.

Cole was a little surprised that she had caught Braxton's attention. It had been awhile since he'd been serious about anyone, especially since he was holding out for the perfect woman. So Londyn must be pretty special. Cole hadn't met her yet, but knew she was a psychologist.

"I say don't give up on Malaya. Everybody who knows both of you can easily see that you two are feelin' each other. I know you say you *really like her,* but I think it's more than that. I've never seen you pursue a woman the way you've been pursuing her."

"Yeah, I know. There's just something about her."

What he felt when he's with Malaya was like nothing Cole had ever felt for a woman, and they hadn't even gone on an official date yet. He couldn't put his finger on what the difference was with her, but he wanted to explore every aspect of Malaya.

"If it's any consolation, I've seen the way she steals glances at you when we're at the bar and she thinks no one is watching." Braxton clapped him on the shoulder as they strolled into the locker room. "Hang in there and take this opportunity to get to know her better. Work that Machine-Gun Cole magic on her, and she'll be begging you to marry her."

Cole laughed. "Yeah, if only it was that easy."

As he showered and changed, Cole thought about what Braxton said. This was definitely a good time to get to know Malaya better.

He was used to going after what he wanted headfirst, but maybe it wouldn't be so bad to take his time with her. It could actually be fun.

CHAPTER NINE

The next day, Cole pulled into the parking lot of Malaya's apartment complex. He was picking her up for the housewarming party, and if it weren't for her, he'd skip it. He wasn't in the mood to be around a bunch of lovey-dovey people.

After finding a parking space, Cole sat in his car and glanced around. It wasn't the best neighborhood, especially for a single woman, but Malaya insisted it was safe. She also liked that it was conveniently located to school. Still, he hated the area.

He climbed out of his Lexus and locked it as he continued checking out his surroundings. There were several guys hanging out on the front stoop of the ten-story brick building smoking and talking loudly. Rap music blared from somewhere inside the building, probably disturbing everyone inside.

Definitely not a place for a single woman.

If only she'd go along with his marriage idea, she wouldn't have to worry about living in substandard conditions.

Cole nodded to the guys outside, then climbed the rickety stairs to the third floor. The tiled hallway appeared as if it hadn't been swept or mopped in weeks, and the dingy walls could stand a fresh coat of paint. All of that only added to his previous opinion of the place.

He stopped at the last door on the right and knocked. Seconds later, after undoing several locks, Malaya swung open the door.

"Hi," she said, a shy smile on her tempting red lips.

She was dressed in a flowy red dress that skimmed over her shapely figure, and black strappy three-inch heels covered her delicate feet. And God, whatever fragrance she was wearing had Cole wanting to bury his nose into the curve of her neck for a better whiff.

His gaze took in her outfit again and worked its way back up. She had removed some of her silver earrings and all of her bracelets. Also gone was her afro. Instead she had straightened her hair, and the long strands brushed her shoulders.

"You don't like it." It was more of a statement rather than a question, and the disappointment in her tone made Cole realize he was frowning.

"It's not that I don't like it. It's—"

"It's what?" she asked. "You know what? Maybe you should come in." She opened the door wider, and he crossed the threshold.

"This," he waved his hand up and down her body, trying to find the right words that could explain what he was thinking without hurting her feelings. "This is not you. It's not your style."

"Oookay, but does it look all right for me to wear? My style isn't dressy enough. I figured that was why… Hold up. Why did you have the outfit delivered to me if you didn't like it?"

"I didn't have…wait. Is this one of the dresses you picked out when you went shopping?"

"Yeah, but you should…" Malaya jammed her hands onto her hips. "If you didn't send it…"

"Dani," they said at the same time.

"I told her I couldn't afford it."

"And when you wouldn't let me pay for the items, she must've taken it upon herself to purchase them," Cole finished. Knowing his sister, he'd probably still end up paying for it.

Which was fine with him. Apparently, Malaya must have liked it. Otherwise, Dani wouldn't have bothered.

"That girl," Malaya said, shaking her head.

Beneath his sister's tough exterior was a gentle woman who loved doing things for others.

"I guess her kind gesture doesn't matter since you don't like the outfit."

"Sweetheart, the dress is pretty and it's stunning on you. It's just not you, and neither is the hairstyle."

She ran her fingers through her tresses. "I guess I was trying too hard to look nice for you and your friends."

Cole cupped her cheek, loving the softness of her skin. "You impress me with who you are and how hard you've been working to reach your goals."

"But I don't want to embarrass you."

"That would never happen. You could wear a potato sack and still be the hottest looking woman I've ever met. As for the people I work with, you don't have to impress them. I'm crazy about you and that's all that matters."

Her left brow rose, and a slow smile crept across her lips. Lips he intended to taste again before the night was over.

"A potato sack?"

He grinned and shrugged. "What can I say? You look good in whatever you wear. But why don't you put on something that you'll be comfortable in."

She glanced down at the dress, a dress that could rival Marilyn Monroe's iconic white dress. It fit perfectly, and she seemed comfortable enough, but Cole knew her. She'd be more at ease in her own style.

"Okay, give me ten minutes."

Malaya turned and headed to the bedroom that was only twenty feet away. Cole watched her every step, admiring the way the outfit hugged her butt. Maybe he'd been too quick to suggest she change clothes. The short dress and high heels put her long, shapely legs on full display. Legs he could envision wrapped around his waist while he thrust...

Whoa. Slow your roll, dude.

He planned to be a perfect gentleman tonight and thoughts like that would definitely get him into trouble. This would be their first official date, and Cole wanted it to be the first of many.

He glanced around Malaya's six-hundred-square-feet of space that was well defined. Though the one-bedroom, one-bathroom was small, it was warm and cozy, but it really didn't reflect her personal style. The living room barely had enough space for the blue tweed sofa, cocktail table, and small television stand. And only one person could fit in the kitchen at a time, but she managed to squeeze in a tiny table and two chairs.

Cole heard Malaya coming before he saw her. She strolled into the living room with an air of confidence that was so her. Her silver jewelry was back in place, including all of her earrings and her fifty million bracelets.

An involuntary smile spread across his face. This was the woman he had fallen for.

Her afro might be temporarily gone, but he liked how she had pulled her hair up into a messy, but sexy bun at the top of her head. Long, curly tendrils of hair framed her face. She had also changed into one of her usual flowery blouses that had a deep V-neck and buttoned in the front. To his delight, the body-hugging garment showed off her full breasts and flat abs. The tail of the shirt was shoved into a pair of black, bell bottom pants that fit snug around her hips and thighs. Cole couldn't see the shoes, but they had to be about three-inch heels since her forehead was in line with his nose.

"Is this better?" she asked, her hands on her hips. The move caused the blouse to stretch across her breasts and revealed a peek of her black lace bra.

Cole met her eyes. She really was a beautiful, sexy woman. "You look amazing."

She rewarded him with a brilliant smile and his heart did a cartwheel inside of his chest.

"Shall we go?" he asked.

"Or we can skip the party and just—"

"Don't even try it. We're going. Do we need to stop and pick up a gift on the way?"

Cole shook his head. "They requested their guest donate to Children's Hospital in lieu of a housewarming gift. I took care of the donation this morning."

"Wow, what a great idea. I guess that means they didn't need anything for their house."

Cole was a hundred percent sure they didn't. Knowing that couple, they probably had enough to furnish several places. He worked with the wife, and the husband was a pediatric surgeon.

Malaya grabbed her handbag and jacket, and they left the apartment. When they made it to the stairs, Cole automatically reached for her hand. She gave him another smile, and his heart practically burst out of his chest. Pride swirled inside of him as he escorted her past the guys, not missing the appreciative gazes his woman was getting.

His woman.

Cole's chest puffed out at the thought. Since they were officially dating, she was his. Maybe going to the party and showing off his stunning date wouldn't be so bad after all.

*

Malaya laughed as Cole drove them to his coworker's home in Buckhead, an upscale Atlanta neighborhood. He told one story after another about when he and Dani were kids. They were close now, and it sounded as if they were even closer back then. Partners in crime.

"My sister is loyal to a fault, but she's also a pain in the ass. I'm sure you already know that, though. I can't tell you how many times I got into trouble because of her." He shook his head and laughed, and Malaya could feel the fondness he had for Dani. "She might've been the source of many headaches and drama, but she was also the one who got me out of jams with our parents."

As he continued sharing their antics, Malaya snuggled deeper into the buttery-soft leather seat. It had been years since she rode in luxury, and she was enjoying how the seat seem to wrap around her body.

"You guys are lucky you have each other. I always wanted a brother and a sister growing up," she said. "Some people might like being an only child, but I hated it. Every day I looked forward to going to school just so I could hang out with my friends. Some I even claimed as family."

"Oh, so you had play cousins too, huh?" Cole cracked, and Malaya couldn't help but laugh.

"Didn't everyone? Since both of my parents were only children, and their extended family is pretty small, I had to claim me some cousins. Otherwise, my childhood really would've been lonely."

"Is that why you want at least three children?" he asked, splitting his attention between her and the road.

Malaya nodded, remembering their conversation over dinner the other day. Little had she known that his question about where she saw herself in five years was a prelude for a bigger question.

"I never wanted Destiny to grow up as an only child. Yet, at the rate I'm going, that's exactly what might happen."

"I guess that means Todd and his wife don't have any children."

"No. They tried a few times, but each pregnancy ended in a miscarriage." Malaya might not like Selena, but she wouldn't wish infertility on anyone. "Destiny said they were talking about adopting her a brother or sister, but that hasn't happened yet."

"Well, you could always accept my offer and we..." his words trailed off and he cursed under his breath. "Forget I said anything."

"Cole—"

"No, I promised myself I wouldn't pressure you, especially not this evening." He reached for her hand and linked his fingers with hers. "It's our first date. I don't want to scare you away discussing marriage and children."

Her heart did funny things when he talked about her, marriage, and children in the same sentence. He not only was

75

willing to marry her, but was even entertaining the idea of having children together.

"You wouldn't scare me away, and I don't want you to think that I don't appreciate your offer. It's beyond generous and selfless, and most women would jump at the chance at being Mrs. Cole Eubanks."

Malaya knew that for a fact, considering the number of women who came on to Cole at the bar. Since knowing him, she'd only seen him with one woman, and that was when she'd first started working at Double Trouble. Dani had called his girlfriend a nutcase at the time, and said that she hoped it wouldn't take Cole a long time to realize it. The two only dated a couple of months.

"For the record, there's only one woman I want and she's sitting next to me."

"You're such a sweet talker."

He brought her hand to his lips and kissed it. "I only speak the truth."

God, this man.

Malaya wanted so badly to go along with his proposition. She was tired of being alone and longed for the day that she'd be able to share her life with someone special. Even though Todd had ruined her trust in men, Cole was allowing her to see that there were still some good guys out there.

If only she and he were in love. Then Malaya would leap at the opportunity. Then again, she thought she had been in love with her ex and look how that turned out.

People get married for all types of reasons. Cole had said.

He was right, but could she really marry someone she wasn't madly and passionately in love with…again?

Cole made a left turn on a tree-lined street and they crept past one large property after another as he searched for his coworker's address.

"Ah, here we go."

The stylish and sleek home sat far back from the street and sported a double-wide circular drive. "Wow, they even have a casita," Malaya said, referring to the smaller home behind the main house.

As they drove toward the home, cars were parked along the driveway. Cole pulled behind a candy-apple-red BMW. "Sit tight. I'll get your door."

Malaya watched as he strolled around the front of the car, looking just as handsome as usual. He had opted for a brown tweed sports jacket, beige turtleneck and brown pants. At his office, the few men she had seen had been clean shaven with their hair cut close to their heads. Not Cole, though. Not only was he sporting an afro, he also had a full beard. She liked the look, especially since he kept both well-groomed.

Cole opened the passenger door and extended his hand. "My lady," he said gallantly, and Malaya's insides quivered as he helped her out of the car.

She already knew dating Cole was going to be fun. They might not be on the same level financially or socially, but he never made her feel as if she was in a lower class. At least not yet. Her and Todd's relationship started similarly, with him treating her like she was the most important person in his world. That lasted awhile, but it hadn't taken long for her to experience his controlling side. Malaya hadn't minded too much in the beginning, but it soon got old.

As she and Cole strolled hand in hand toward to the stately home, she wondered if it would be like that with him. Would he eventually turn controlling? Would he do whatever he wanted in their relationship—her opinions be damned?

Malaya didn't think so, but time would tell.

"Welcome. Welcome," a tall, older woman with shocking red hair and freckles covering much of her fair skin said when she opened the door. "Cole, I was wondering if you were going to show up, and who is this lovely lady?"

Before Cole could respond, the woman was joined by a man who was just as tall, with dark skin and a disarming smile. "Baby, let them in the house before you start interrogating," he said.

They all laughed and Cole slid his arm around Malaya as they crossed the threshold.

"Chris and Katherine, I want you to meet Malaya Radcliff. Malaya, these are the rich folks who own this massive home." He glanced around. "Or should I say mansion? Clearly, I need to have Katherine start investing for me."

"Whatever." She waved him off and looped her arm with Malaya's. "It's nice to meet you. I'm sure you had everything to do with Cole being here. So, thanks for that." Her warm smile made Malaya feel even more comfortable. "Come on. Let us show you both around."

What stood out immediately was the huge crystal chandelier hanging between the dual spiral staircase. The outside of the home was impressive, but the jaw-dropping decor on the inside was like something out of *House Beautiful.*

For the next thirty minutes, the couple took them from one huge room to the next. Cathedral ceilings, shiny hardwood floors, wall-to-wall windows, and a to-die-for kitchen were only a few of the highlights for Malaya. The seven-bedroom, ten-bathroom estate was one of the most spectacular homes she had ever been in. That was saying a lot, since her ex-in-laws lived in a stately mansion.

An hour into the party, people were still showing up, and Malaya was fascinated by the group. She half expected for Cole's coworkers to be like Todd's extended family, thinking they were better than the average Joe. That wasn't the case at all. They were down-to-earth and treated each other like family.

Malaya was in the enormous dining room where several food stations were set up. She was stuffed, but couldn't stop herself from getting another red velvet cheesecake cupcake. They were like heaven on earth.

"Are you having a good time?" Valerie asked, also seeming to have a sweet tooth as she loaded a small plate up with dessert.

"I am. What about you?"

She nodded. "Yes, and I've made a total pig of myself." They both laughed. "More than that, though, I'm in awe of this lovely home."

They chatted for a few minutes, each discussing their

favorite rooms. Malaya could see why Cole was so fond of his assistant. She was easygoing and had a fun sense of humor. She also seemed full of life with her wicked one-liners and hearty laugh.

"I'm surprised Cole let you out of his sight. I thought he would hover over you the whole night."

Malaya smiled. She did have to shoo him away a couple of times, insisting that he hang out with some of the guys. Thanks to their amazing hosts and the friendliness of the guests, Malaya felt comfortable roaming around by herself.

"He's a little overprotective and thinks he needs to be by my side in order for me to have a good time."

"That sounds like him. He's such a thoughtful young man."

Malaya's heart swelled. "That he is." No one knew better than her just how thoughtful.

"I can tell Cole is quite taken with you. I'm glad he's finally found someone who makes him happy." Valerie patted her arm and gave her a warm smile. "I'll be heading out soon, but I'm looking forward to seeing you at future events."

Malaya returned her smile and wished her a good evening as she watched Valerie leave the room. To her, Cole always seemed happy. Then again, his assistant would know better since she was around him often.

As Malaya went in search of him, she noted there was something else that was very clear among the people from his job. They were big on family. In addition to finance, family had been the gist of much of the conversation. From what she could tell, Cole might've been the only one who wasn't married with kids, or at least engaged.

Had that been why he'd asked her to marry him? Surely, he wasn't concerned about what this group thought of him still being a bachelor. Then again, maybe it was a big deal.

Malaya's gaze searched the large family room where she had left Cole earlier. She spotted him speaking to two men as they stood near the patio door—if she could call it that. It was actually a sliding glass wall that opened to the massive backyard and overlooked the Olympic-sized swimming pool.

Her gaze traveled the length of Cole's tall frame. Damn, the man was fine. At over six feet, he was taller than the two guys with whom he was engaged in a heated discussion. Malaya had already been in lust with him, but lately, he seemed to stand out even more. His chest seemed wider. His shoulders were broader. His long legs seemed to go on forever. Hell, the man was in a league all his own, and as far as she was concerned, no one else came close.

Damn, I have it bad.

"Girl, don't even waste your time with him."

Malaya startled at the feminine voice behind her. When she glanced over her shoulder, her gaze landed on an Amazon-like woman with skin the color of terra cotta, and deep dark eyes that seemed to look right through Malaya. She was dressed in a royal blue slip dress that left nothing to the imagination and sky-high heels with straps that wrapped around her calves. Instead of a housewarming party, she looked as if she was heading to a nightclub.

"Excuse me?" Malaya finally said.

"I saw you checking out Cole Eubanks. That's a whole lot of man wrapped up in a sexy package, but don't waste your time. His stuck-up ass ain't looking for nothing serious. Besides..." she looked Malaya up and down, "you wouldn't stand a chance."

One of Malaya's brows rose and she tapped down the irritation poking at her nerves. "Is that right? And you would know this how?"

She gave a nonchalant shrug. "Just a hunch. Your seventies vibe is kinda cute, but trust me, you're not Cole's type."

"But you are?"

"Yeah, actually I am."

"I see."

Malaya's attention went back to Cole, and as if he sensed her watching him, he turned his head slightly. Their gazes met. Then he glanced at the woman standing next to her.

"I knew it wouldn't take but a second for him to walk this way," the woman said arrogantly. "He never could resist me in this dress."

Boy, is she in for a surprise, Malaya thought, giddiness bubbling inside of her.

With one hand in his front pocket, Cole wove around groups of people as he headed their way. As he grew close, his long, confident strides added to his larger-than-life persona, and Malaya's heart rate edged up. Yeah, he really was one sexy man.

"Hey, Beautiful." He slid his arm around her back before placing a lingering kiss on her lips.

They hadn't discussed their views on public displays of affection or how she'd be introduced to his friends, and so far, they'd been winging it. But right now, she couldn't have planned this moment better if she had tried.

"You doing all right?" he asked when the kiss ended.

The mystery woman gasped, and Malaya had to keep herself from laughing.

"I am now. I was missing you," she said to Cole in her sexiest voice.

"Wait. You two...are together?" The mystery woman's tone held a level of shock, as if the idea of Malaya with Cole was too ridiculous to believe. The scowl on her face and the way she glared at Malaya would've been comical if she didn't have the look of murder in her eyes.

"I guess you've met Angela," Cole said without a lick of warmth in his tone.

"Not officially, but she did give me a little insight about you." Malaya smoothed her hand lovingly over Cole's cheek. She'd wanted to do that from the moment he started growing his full beard and it was as soft as she'd imagined. "I believe her exact words were 'that's a whole lot of man wrapped in a sexy package.'"

"Is that right?" He was staring down at Malaya, and the left corner of his lips kicked up as humor glimmered in his eyes. "Sexy package, huh?"

"Yup, and I couldn't agree more. She also mentioned that I would never stand a chance with you and that I wasn't your type."

The grin fell from his lips, and he glowered at Angela. "I see you're still spewing venom and stirring up trouble."

Her lips twisted into an evil sneer, and she folded her arms across her chest. "How was I supposed to know you had lowered your standards?"

Cole released a humorless laugh. "See, Angela, that's where you're wrong. If anything, I've upped my standards and finally found a woman worthy of my time."

Angela snorted. "I find it hard to believe that you gave up all this—" she waved a hand up and down her body, "for *her*," she spat, looking at Malaya as if she was dog poop on her red-bottomed heels. "Don't get too comfortable, girlfriend. If you're expecting forever with Cole, you really are wasting your time. He's not the settling-down type."

Cole started to respond, but Malaya stopped him with a hand on his chest.

"Oh, I'm sorry, Angela," she said sweetly. "I probably should've formally introduced myself when you first started judging me. I'm Malaya. The future Mrs. Eubanks."

CHAPTER TEN

Cole was still laughing when they walked into Malaya's apartment. "I thought her eyes were going to fall out of her head when you introduced yourself as the future Mrs. Eubanks."

Malaya grabbed a couple of bottled waters from the refrigerator. "I can't believe I stooped to her level, but I couldn't resist. Someone needed to knock her butt off that pedestal that she had propped herself on."

"And you were the perfect person to do it."

Malaya handed Cole one of the waters, then sat on the sofa next to him. "I hope I didn't make you uncomfortable with what I said. What if some of your coworkers heard?"

He gave a nonchalant shrug. "I'll deal with it. Some of the people who were there know how Angela is. She's attended a few events, which was how I first met her. She's Chris's cousin," he said of the owner of the house. "I should've given you a heads-up that she might be there, but I honestly didn't think about it."

"Did Angela have a high opinion of herself when you two dated?"

"Not initially, or at least I hadn't noticed it at first. By the end, though, I knew she was a few screws short of a hardware store."

Malaya laughed.

"I couldn't get away from her fast enough. She wasn't one of my proudest dating moments. I haven't seen you with anyone, but have you dated much since your divorce?"

"Nope. After that disastrous time in my life, dating was the last thing on my mind." At least until recently, but she kept that thought to herself. "Have you dated a lot?"

"Not lately. After college, I was focused on getting my career off the ground, investing, and just trying to build up my financial portfolio. Once that was on course, I dated often, trying to find a wife."

He chuckled and shook his head with an unreadable expression on his face. Malaya was curious about what he was thinking, but it was safe to assume his search process hadn't gone well. Especially if Angela was any indication.

"I've always wanted to get married and have a family. It's kind of hard not to want that after spending time with my parents. They've always made marriage look easy."

"They're wonderful," Malaya said.

The few times that she'd been around them, they were holding hands, stealing kisses, and staring into each other's eyes. She specifically recalled a moment during Dani's birthday party when she caught them smiling at each other, as if silently sharing a secret. What would it have been like to grow up with parents who shared that type of love? Would she have chosen better when it came to husbands?

"I know I said I wouldn't bring up the proposal again," Cole said, interrupting her thoughts. "But my parents are a good example of having an unconventional marriage."

"What do you mean?"

"They'd only known each other for two months before my father proposed. A couple of weeks later they were married."

Malaya's mouth dropped open. "Are you for real?"

"Yep. That was forty-five years ago. My father said he knew the moment he saw her that she was going to be his wife. My mom said he was full of crap, but his charm was irresistible." Cole laughed.

"Were they in love?"

Cole tilted his head slightly and stared at the wall across the room as if in deep thought. "I know my father was. I'm not sure about my mother. She grew up in an abusive home, and I think initially my dad was her way out."

Malaya nodded.

People get married for all types of reasons. Cole's words from the other day continued playing through her mind. The way he was watching her now had her wondering if he was recalling his words.

"Forty-five years," she said on a wistful sigh. "And they seem madly in love."

Cole pushed a loose strand of Malaya's hair behind her ear. "They are."

Time stood still as she stared into Cole's kind eyes. The evening had been more fun than she'd had in a long time, and it was all because of him.

"I noticed at the party that most of your coworkers are either married or engaged. Does that have anything to do with part of your reason for wanting to marry me?"

Cole released a noisy sigh and leaned back against the sofa. "After my boxing days, I sat down and did a life plan. Kind of a roadmap to what I wanted to accomplish by the time I was forty. I've met all of my benchmarks, except one."

Malaya nodded. Now his proposal was starting to make more sense. She didn't doubt he was trying to help her with her situation, but there would definitely be something in it for him, too.

"I want a family." He slowly ran his hand over his beard as he spoke. "Wife, kids, a backyard, I want it all. It's not just because I'm surrounded by happy, loving couples. I've always imagined myself married with a few children. I just thought it would happen before I turn forty."

"Why forty? What happens if you're forty-five before you marry and start a family?"

Cole's unreadable gaze met hers, but before he responded,

Malaya's cell phone rang.

"Sorry." She leaned forward and picked up the device from the sofa table and glanced at the screen. *Oh, great.* "It's Todd."

Talking to him was the perfect way to ruin a wonderful evening, but she didn't have a choice. As long as Destiny was under his roof, Malaya would pick up every time. Of course, he knew that.

"Hello," she said, and put the phone on speaker.

"Hey, I just wanted you to know that Destiny won't be able to spend this coming weekend with you."

Annoyance simmered inside of Malaya, but she steadied her breathing to keep from snapping. While Todd lived to piss her off, tonight she wouldn't give him the satisfaction. It helped that Cole was sitting next to her; Mr. Cool, Calm, and Collected.

"Todd, you already know I have plans with her. We're looking forward to spending the long weekend together."

Destiny didn't have school Friday and Monday, and Malaya had been glad to know the off days had fallen on her weekend.

"I'm picking her up Thursday night as planned. So please make sure she's ready."

Todd's ruthless laughter filled the quietness of the living room, and Malaya's annoyance quickly turned into anger.

"I don't know who you think you are, but you don't tell me what to do."

"I'm her mother!" Malaya ground out.

She wanted to call him all types of asshole as her temper was drawn tighter than a spring coil, ready to snap at any moment. Cole moved closer to her and draped his arm on the back of the sofa, and his square jaw visibly clenched.

"Todd, I don't want to argue with you, but we have a court-ordered agreement. This coming weekend is my weekend to have Destiny. I already have plans with her."

"Well, I've just changed them," he said with satisfaction, as if what she wanted was no big deal. "Selena and I are taking

Destiny to New York to a Broadway show that she's been wanting to see. This is the only weekend I have available. So, I guess you'll have to make other plans."

"Damn it! You can't do this!" Malaya screamed and pounded her fist on the sofa.

"I can do whatever the hell I want!" he yelled back.

"No, you can't! The courts say that I get her every other weekend, and this is my weekend. If you even think about keeping her away from me, I will take you to—" Malaya stopped abruptly when Cole squeezed her shoulder and shook his head. She hadn't noticed that he had moved even close and she was practically in his lap.

"You will what? Take me to court? Try to get sole custody?" Todd taunted.

Tears filled Malaya's eyes, and her chest heaved as she sat with her fists balled in her lap. It was good that Cole stopped her when he had. There was no sense in giving her ex-husband any more ammunition. He knew she didn't have the means to take him to court, and there were so many aspects of her life that still needed to be in order.

"I'll call Destiny in the morning," Malaya said, her throat clogged with emotion before she disconnected the call.

She buried her face in her hands, no longer able to hold back the sobs that wracked her body.

It wasn't fair. She played by the awful rules that the court had set forth regarding the time she could spend with Destiny, and look where it got her. Nowhere. Todd could do whatever he wanted. He could yank the little time she did have with her daughter away and think nothing of it.

Cole pulled Malaya close and held her tightly.

"I can't do this anymore." Her teary declaration was muffled against his chest. "I can't let him keep getting away with this crap."

"I know, baby," Cole said quietly, and kissed the top of her head. "I know."

Malaya didn't know how long they held their position, but by the time she lifted her head, she was ready to fight back.

Cole stuffed a few tissues into her hand.

"Thank you, and I'm sorry about all of this. I never wanted to pull you into my drama."

He reached out and caressed her cheek with the pad of his thumb. It was so tender and comforting, Malaya was afraid she'd start crying all over again.

"No apology necessary," he said. "It pisses me the hell off knowing that you have to go through this with that asshole. I wish there was something more I could do to help."

Malaya studied him and didn't miss the sincerity in his eyes. Even with her fractured heart, having him by her side and wanting to help her meant everything.

She sat back on the sofa and looped her arm through his before laying her head on his shoulder. Finally knowing what she had to do, she released a contented breath.

"Does your offer of marriage still stand?"

*

The next afternoon, Cole and Malaya were sitting in Randall's office, discussing next steps relating to getting married and preparing for a custody battle. The plan was to petition the court for joint custody, though Malaya was adamant about eventually going after Todd for sole custody.

First, they needed to get married.

"I'm not entering the marriage with anything. So, I don't expect anything when it ends," Malaya said.

"Look at me," Cole said gently and waited patiently for her to turn to him. He understood that she was operating on very little sleep from the night before, thanks to Todd's phone call, but enough was enough. "We need to get something straight once and for all. This is not some fake marriage. I told you and Randall that. We are not going into this union thinking it's going to end."

Randall rocked in his high-backed desk chair as he tapped his ink pen on the desk. "If that's the case, why do you guys need a marriage contract?"

"Because I want one," Malaya said. "Cole is giving up everything. I know he's trying to be optimistic, but I don't want him going into this marriage without being protected."

Cole threw up his hands and huffed out a breath. "Sweetheart, I think we're about to have our first argument because I don't know how many times I have to tell you that—"

"I know what you said, but you have never been married. It's so much more than saying 'I do.' It's so much more than liking or loving someone. Marriage takes a lot of work. Besides, you haven't lived with anyone since college. You don't even know if we'll get along."

"Actually, we're going to get along just fine. Will we have disagreements? Probably. But we are two mature adults who care about each other. Neither of us will say or do anything that will disrespect or hurt the other."

"You don't know that," she said quietly, some of the fight edging out of her.

Cole reached for her hand and held it. "I *do* know that. Keep in mind, we've been friends a while now, and with that has come respect. You're not marrying someone you just met off the street. You're agreeing to marry someone who absolutely adores you, and I'd bet my paycheck that you feel the same way about me."

A ghost of a smile played around her sweet lips, but she didn't respond. She didn't have to. He could see it in her eyes each time she looked at him that she cared deeply.

"Also, stop comparing what you and I share to what you and Todd had. He was an idiot to ever let you go. I won't make that mistake."

Without releasing her hand, Cole glanced at his friend, who was sitting on the other side of the desk. "Randall, since my future wife is adamant about us having a marriage contract, this is what I want in it. *If*—and that's a big *if*—we ever get divorced, she gets half of every single thing I have."

Malaya shook her head vigorously. "No. Randall, don't listen to—"

"*And,*" Cole interrupted, "put this in the document. She has to cook for me at least twice a week. We'll figure out the other days. Oh, and after one year of marriage, if not sooner, I want us to have a baby."

Malaya's eyes rounded and her mouth formed a perfect "O," and Cole continued telling Randall what he wanted in the contract.

"She can work if she wants to. She can even go back to school for her masters. I'll support her financially, mentally, emotionally…whatever she wants or needs, I'll support her. You got that?" he asked Randall, but Cole's gaze was steady on Malaya. He wanted her to see how serious he was about their marriage.

"Got it," Randall piped up, humor in his voice. "Anything else?"

Cole sat back in his seat. "I think that's it for me, now it's Laya's turn."

She stared at him for the longest time before speaking. "Whatever Cole comes to the marriage with will still be his if our marriage doesn't work."

Cole couldn't stop the grin that spread across his face. "Did you get that, Randall? She said *if*, not when, but *if*. I think I'm making progress. She's finally understanding that once we say 'I do,' it's a done deal. We're playing for keeps, and divorce is not an option."

Malaya rolled her eyes and turned her attention to Randall, who wore a smirk on his face. "I just can't with him."

Randall laughed. "You don't know the half of it. You're about to marry one of the most stubborn people I know. Only second to his sister, Dani, but I will say this—Cole is solid. He'll treat you right on every front, and I'm not just saying that because we're friends."

Malaya nodded and squeezed Cole's thigh. "I know. I just hope I can make him happy."

"You've already made me happy by agreeing to marry me."

"What else would you like in the contract, Malaya?" Randall asked.

"And don't say *nothing*," Cole said. "Otherwise, we're not

leaving until you come up with something."

"And if you two are still here in an hour, I'm charging triple my hourly rate."

Malaya gasped. "You wouldn't!"

"The hell if he won't," Cole cracked. "So, let's get this done and get out of here. Now, what else? Though I'm serious about divorce not being an option, what else would you want from me? And remember, I'm not Todd. No matter what happens in the future, you and your well-being will always be important to me."

Malaya nibbled on her bottom lip, and Cole could almost hear the gears in her head turning. He thought the contract was pointless, but it did give him a chance to throw in the baby idea. He honestly thought she would shoot down the request. Especially since she had the next couple of her years mapped out, but she hadn't said a word.

"I want your word that we'll try and get full custody of Destiny."

"That goes without saying."

"And I want the townhouse and your Lexus."

Now Cole was the one stunned. Not that he wouldn't give her anything she wanted, he was just surprised that's what she came up with. "Done. Anything else?" he asked.

She cleared her throat and ran her palms up and down her jean-clad thighs. "No. I think that's it."

Cole stood and pulled Malaya up with him. "Write it up, Randall, and keep the part about her getting half of whatever I have in there."

She *tsk*ed. "Cole."

"Don't say anything." He wrapped his arms around her waist and pulled her against his body. "I'm going to prove to you that all husbands aren't assholes. All I ask is that you give me a fair chance."

"Okay," she said quietly. "I'm counting on you to show me."

Cole covered her mouth with his and devoured its softness, loving the way Malaya slid her hand behind his head to deepen their connection. He tuned out Randall's mumbling about them getting out of his office, and focused solely on his future wife.

He already couldn't get enough of her and looked forward to showing her how a husband was supposed to cherish his wife.

CHAPTER ELEVEN

Malaya was bubbling with excitement and almost leaped into Cole's arms the moment he opened the door. The only thing that stopped her was him standing in a dark suit looking absolutely delicious while holding two champagne flutes.

"Congratulations, sweetheart," he crooned and her face split into a wide grin.

"Aww, Cole. Thank you."

He stepped back and let her enter the hallway of the townhouse.

"Set your bag on the step for a minute."

Malaya did as he asked, and then he handed her one of the champagne glasses.

"Now, come here." He slid his arm around her waist. "Before we make a toast, there's something I've been looking forward to doing all day."

Cole's lips touched hers, and Malaya knew she would never get tired of his sweet kisses. Since leaving his lawyer's office the day before, they'd been finding every opportunity and reason to share a kiss.

She hadn't moved in yet, but this was how she wanted to end a school and work day. Coming home to quietness and being loved on by her man. No walking through cigarette smoke to get to her apartment. No loud rap music blaring the moment she pulled into the apartment parking lot. And no upstairs or downstairs neighbors arguing loud enough to make her feel as if they were inside her apartment.

God, I can get used to all of this, she thought.

"Definitely worth the wait," Cole mumbled against her mouth before ending the kiss.

"I agree," Malaya said, giving him another quick peck.

Cole dropped his arm from around her and lifted his glass.

"Seems this week has come with a lot to celebrate, and before we go upstairs, I want to make a toast. To the most amazing woman I know who is slaying life one day at a time. Congratulations on the new job, baby. I have no doubt that you're going to help take the company to the next level."

Malaya tapped her glass to his and sipped her champagne. She felt as if her heart would explode from all of the excitement she'd been experiencing lately. First agreeing to marry Cole, and then the interview.

She had met with Supreme Security earlier in the day, and they hired her on the spot. Malaya figured Cole's endorsement helped, but she gave herself some of the credit. She had gone into the interview more than prepared and was able to answer their questions easily, while also showcasing that she had done her research. She probably knew more about their company than most of their other employees. One of the highlights of the interview was meeting a few of their security personnel, or as Hamilton referred to them—*Atlanta's Finest.* All of them had law enforcement backgrounds, everything from police officers to former FBI agents. Some were even former military. Not only were the men absolutely gorgeous, but they exuded strength and power.

"I want to hear all about it," Cole said as he followed her up the stairs.

Malaya had called him the moment she left Supreme, barely able to contain her enthusiasm. It felt so good to be able to share her news with someone who actually cared. There were moments throughout the day where it still didn't feel real that she had landed a job. Especially after trying for months to get companies to even notice her.

She took another sip of the champagne and headed up to the main level where she left her overnight bag near the stairs. For the next few minutes, they stood in the kitchen as she recapped her morning. After the interview, she'd only had a few minutes to get to school, and had barely made it in time. Her car had stopped on her twice, but she kept that information to herself.

"It had been so long since I'd interviewed, I might've been over prepared." She laughed.

"I am so proud of you."

There was awe in Cole's voice as he spoke those words. Malaya felt so lucky to have his support. The way he listened and the quiet assurance of his presence made her feel as if she could take on the world.

"I couldn't have gotten that job without you."

Cole shook his head as he loosened his tie. It was one of Malaya's favorites with swirls of purple, orange, yellow, brown, and beige.

"All I did was make a phone call. You're the one who landed the job. You're the one who went in there and showed them that you're the best person for the position. They're going to love working with you."

His faith in her never ceased to amaze her. She stepped forward and with her hands on his hard chest, she raised up on tiptoes.

"I'm going to love being your wife," she said, and kissed him.

Malaya wanted him to feel how much she appreciated him, how much she adored him. It might have taken her a while to embrace the marriage idea, but now that she had, she was going to enjoy every moment with her man.

When the kiss ended, Cole cupped her face as if he was going to kiss her again. Instead he said, "I'm going to love being your husband. Speaking of being your husband, I talked to Mason Bennett a couple of hours ago."

"Oh, about having our reception at his club?"

Mason was not only the owner of Supreme Security, but he and his siblings also owned Club Masquerade, one the hottest nightclubs in Atlanta. They were usually closed on Sunday afternoons, and Cole thought it would be a good spot to have a small reception.

"What did he say?"

"He said he'd check with his sister who oversees events there, but he didn't think it would be a problem."

"Are you sure it'll be okay having Destiny at a nightclub?"

"I'm positive. We'll be there during the afternoon when it's not opened to the public."

Though they picked up the marriage license after leaving Randall's office the day before, they planned to wait a couple of weeks before getting married. Malaya wanted Destiny to be a part of the celebration. So instead of getting married on a weekday at the courthouse, they'd wait until the next time she was scheduled to have her daughter. They'd have a small, intimate wedding that Sunday afternoon, and the reception that evening.

The only thing or person who could throw off their plans was Todd. Cole had said if her ex tried any shady stuff, they'd deal with him. She wasn't sure exactly what that meant, but it felt good to have Cole in her corner.

"Oh, and the club will also take care of the catering, so we won't have to worry about that," he added. "Okay, enough about the wedding details. Let's get this celebration started. Well, after I get out of this suit. I just ordered the pizza, but are you sure you don't want me to take you to a restaurant?"

"I'm positive. It's been a busy day and I'm looking forward to a nice, quiet evening here with you."

"All right, kick off your shoes and get comfortable. We should be able to find a movie on cable or Netflix. If not, I'll have to come up with another way to entertain my beautiful fiancée."

Malaya giggled when he wiggled his brows. She wondered what his form of entertainment would look like.

"I'll be back shortly."

"I'll be here."

So, this is what it'll be like to come home to him, Malaya thought as she watched him head for the stairs. He carried her overnight bag upstairs with him, and she wondered which room he'd put it in—the second guest room, or his?

"I guess I'll find out," she murmured under her breath and dropped down on the leather sofa.

As she toed off her shoes, she glanced around the large room. The day before, Cole had told her she had free rein on changing anything she wanted to in the house, except for his office. That space was off-limits. But so far, there wasn't a thing she'd change, except for the second guest room. That would eventually be Destiny's room.

Malaya grabbed the remote and started flipping through channels while she waited for Cole. She was pretty sure he wouldn't be interested in a chick flick, but one of her favorites was on.

"Okay, the pizza should be here in a few minutes," he said as he strolled into the living room.

Her gaze raked over him and suddenly she wasn't just hungry for pizza. Damn, the man was built. He had changed into a black T-shirt that stretched across his muscular chest and hugged his large biceps. Malaya's attention traveled lower to the gray sweatpants that hung low on his hips, and suddenly, her whole body was pulsing with need. She used to think that sweatpants on a well-endowed man should be outlawed, but that was before she saw them on her man.

Good Lord.

The way the material emphasized his huge package had her squeezing her thighs together as a pool of luscious heat catapulted through her body.

"You like what you see?"

Malaya's gaze leaped to his eyes and warmth spread to her cheeks, knowing that he had caught her gawking at his junk. Part of her was mortified, but the part of her that hadn't had sex in like forever wanted to keep staring.

"I do," she said boldly. Soon they'd be married. She'd have

to get used to his hot body.

Cole's brows quirked up and a sexy grin spread across his juicy lips. Maybe she'd had too much champagne, but right now, she wanted to jump her man's bones and have him buried inside of her.

"Sweetheart, if you keep looking at me like that, I'm going to throw you over my shoulder and carry you to my bedroom. *Our* bedroom."

Technically, it wasn't *theirs* yet, but Malaya's heart rate skyrocketed at the idea of sex with Cole, her soon-to-be husband.

I'm getting married.

I'm marrying Cole.

Considering how she'd initially shot down the idea, she was ready to shout it to the world.

"What—what about the pizza?" she asked weakly.

Cole froze mid-step. "Woman, don't play with me. I've wanted you for so long, I don't give a damn about pizza. Hell, I'll even leave a note and a hefty tip outside if it means having you right now."

The doorbell rang and Malaya wasn't sure if she should be happy or pissed by the interruption.

Pissed. Definitely pissed.

Curiosity was getting the best of her, and her body was starving for some male attention. But was she ready to go all the way with Cole? Yes, they were getting married in a couple of weeks. Yet, they hadn't really discussed the more intimate parts of marriage.

Specifically, sex.

This is not some fake marriage. Cole's words from the day before rattled through her brain.

The doorbell rang again, and Cole said, "Don't move. This conversation isn't over." He hurried to the door and, within seconds, was back with an extra-large pizza. "Now, where were we?"

"You were talking about taking me upstairs and having your way with me," Malaya said with more sass than she actually felt. She was talking a good game, flirting with her future husband, but could she back it up?

He set the pizza box on the table in front of the sofa. "That's right, I was. Then let's do this."

Malaya gasped when he scooped her off the sofa and swung her up in his arms as if she weighed nothing.

"So, um, you're serious?" she asked as he carried her to the stairs.

Cole's gorgeous light-brown eyes sparked with desire, and her insides melted.

"I'm dead serious, but if you're not ready—"

"I'm ready," Malaya said quickly. "I'm more than ready."

CHAPTER TWELVE

The moment Cole laid her on the huge bed, he climbed on top of her and kissed her with a hunger that rivaled all of their other kisses. Passion pulsed through Malaya with every lap of his tongue and his heady cologne aroused a desire that had laid dormant within her for years. Every one of her senses were on high alert, and the throbbing need between her thighs grew more needy.

She wanted him so bad, wanted all of him. Yet, it didn't matter that her arms were wrapped tightly around his neck and their bodies were so close that light couldn't be seen between them. It wasn't enough. She wanted to feel all of him.

As if reading her mind, Cole snatched his mouth from hers. "I need you out of these clothes," he said, panting.

She hurried into a sitting position, and he had her T-shirt over her head and tossed to the floor within seconds. Next went her yoga pants that ended up with the discarded shirt. That left her in a simple purple bra and black cotton bikinis. Had she known that she'd end up in bed with him, she would've chosen sexier underwear. Then again, the way Cole's appreciative gaze crawled over her, maybe it didn't matter.

Her body shivered. It wasn't that she was cold—far from it—but there was an intensity in his penetrating gaze that hadn't been there a moment ago.

"I wondered if you had piercings anywhere else." He gently fingered the diamond stud that was through her naval. "I like this. Does it hurt when I touch it?"

"Not at all. Feel free to touch every part of me."

"I plan to." He bent down and nipped at her chin and worked his way back up to her lips. "I know we're getting married, but I want to make something very clear before we cross this line. You're mine. There's no turning back. *You're mine.* Got it?"

Malaya nodded. As worked up as he had her, she was about ready to agree to anything. She was more than ready to consummate their relationship. Sure, they could wait a couple of weeks until after they were married, but she wanted him now. She wanted him more than she'd ever wanted any man, including her ex.

"The soon-to-be Mrs. Colton Eubanks," Cole continued, torturing her with tender kisses down her neck and onto her bare shoulders. "It's me and you...forever." He peppered more kisses across the swell of her breasts. "No turning back. No..."

Malaya grabbed his face with both of her hands and forced him to look at her. "Stop talking and make love to me."

Cole's megawatt smile stoked the fire that was already burning out of control within her. "It would be my pleasure."

He quickly slipped out of his clothes, putting his incredible body on full display. Malaya had been dumbstruck seeing him in the gray sweatpants, but with all of his rippling muscles and his nakedness standing next to the bed, the man had her speechless. There wasn't a lick of fat anywhere on his body.

He pulled open the nightstand drawer, oblivious to her ogling him. His muscles contracted with each move he made and the scene was almost hypnotizing. If her body was as fit as his was, Malaya would never wear clothing. At least, not much.

Cole tossed a couple of foil packets on top of the nightstand, then climbed back onto the bed. Once Malaya was rid of her underwear, she was about ready to leap out of her skin. She couldn't wait any longer, especially now with the way Cole was checking her out.

Malaya swallowed and tried not to squirm as her insides quivered. She felt like the most beautiful woman in the world. From the first time they kissed, he had awakened a passion in her that she could barely contain. And now...

"Ohh," she moaned and her back arched when Cole's cold fingertip glided down the center of her body, searing a path from her neck to the swell of her breasts.

"You have no idea what you do to me," he said huskily.

If what she did to him was anything like what he was doing to her, she knew.

"You're absolutely breathtaking," he continued, still staring.

"You are, too."

Cole straddled her and cupped her breasts with both hands, squeezing them together before his mouth covered a pert nipple. Malaya moaned with every lap and swirl of his tongue. The way he sucked and teased had her wiggling beneath him. If he kept this up, she was going to come before they even got started good.

But she loved it.

Loved the sweet torture of his mouth on her body. It was impossible to control the powerful desire raging through her, nipping at every nerve when he was so thorough.

Malaya's hand went behind his head, holding him in place as he worshipped one breast, then the other one. She already knew how masterful his mouth was, but he wielded his tongue around each nipple better than a gunslinger handled a gun. Her heart was pounding so hard and fast it felt as if it would beat right out of her chest.

"Man, baby," Cole said roughly, his face buried between her breasts. "You smell and feel so damn good, I'm about to explode. I need to be inside of you."

He lifted up and made quick work of sheathing himself. Malaya's gaze was glued to his erection, admiring how huge he was as he nudged her legs apart. His penis bumped against her sex, sending a whole new wave of desire pumping through her veins.

This was happening. This was really happening. Excitement and anxiousness warred inside of her.

"Relax," Cole crooned and lowered his head to kiss her. While his mouth made love to hers, one of his hands glided down her side and stopped at her hip. "I love kissing you," he rasped when he lifted his head slightly. "And I know I'm going to enjoy making love to you."

He slowly entered her, and Malaya sucked in a breath, willing herself to relax and allow her body to adjust to his size. He was so long, thick, and hard and...

Cole stopped moving, and Malaya's eyes bore into him. She wanted to scream—*don't you dare stop!* But she didn't have to. Whatever he saw on her face caused him to smirk and he slid in even deeper.

He felt so good.

Her sex tightened around his length as his hips started rotating, and he moved inside of her with smooth, even strokes. Before long, he picked up speed. Going faster. Deeper. Harder. Malaya matched his moves as pressure quickly built inside of her.

"Co—Cole," she panted, struggling for air as her hands slid down his sweat-slicked back and then gripped his taut butt. He continued thrusting in and out of her like a man possessed.

She was so close to her release. So clo...

"Cole!" she shrieked.

Malaya's body bucked uncontrollably against him when an orgasm ripped from her and shoved her over the edge of control. As she struggled to catch her breath, her head thrashed back and forth against the pillow as a hot tide rolled through her body.

Cole was relentless. He didn't let up. He continued pumping his hips, picking up speed with every thrust as he neared his release.

Seconds later, his body stiffened and a guttural growl tore through the bedroom moments before he collapsed on top of her.

"Ahh, man...damn," he wheezed, his voice muffled against her neck as his body shook.

She wrapped her arms around him as they rode the aftershocks together. His weight was practically crushing her, but Malaya didn't care. She held him close, her chest heaving against him as their breaths mingled.

A deep satisfaction settled inside of her. Making love with him was just as amazing as she had fantasized about.

Cole eventually rolled onto his back still gasping for air, and when his hand blindly found hers, he squeezed. No words were spoken between them. None were needed. The intensity of what they'd just experienced made Malaya look forward to the next round.

In the meantime, her eyes drifted shut and that was her last thought when sleep overpowered her.

*

Cole stared down at the sleeping beauty who he planned to spend the rest of his life with. It was six o'clock in the morning, and though he was exhausted, he knew he had to get moving. What he wanted more than anything, though, was to stay in bed and continue familiarizing himself with Malaya's body.

After three intense rounds that spilled over into the morning, he probably should let her rest, but they didn't have that luxury. He needed to get to work, and she had class in a couple of hours. But man, he was going to be grinning like an idiot for the rest of the day.

After the first round of sex, they had drifted off, but woke up and had cold pizza in bed. That gave them the energy to go another round, and it had been just as passionate as the first.

Cole bent over Malaya and nibbled on her ear, then trailed feathery kisses down her scented neck. He didn't think he would ever get enough of her.

"Mmm," she moaned, the sound making him hard all over again. She twisted and stretched her arms up and out, causing the bedsheet to slide down her curvy frame and put her full breasts on display.

Down, boy, Cole told his body as his eyes gobbled her up. There would be plenty of time for more lovemaking, he'd see to that, but right now, he had to get her up.

"How about some coffee to get your day started?" he said, knowing the mention of coffee would wake her. As expected, her head jerked up, almost headbutting him in the process. Cole chuckled. "I'll take that as a yes."

Malaya sluggishly sat up, still looking exhausted, and slowly propped herself against the upholstered headboard. She gave Cole a shy smile and wrapped the sheet around herself before he handed her the steaming mug of coffee.

Would he ever get used to them being together? Soon, he'd be able to wake up next to her every day, see her, touch her, and make love to her. The thought of that seemed so unreal.

Malaya took a tentative sip of the steaming brew and moaned. She had no idea how the sound affected him. If she did, she'd stop making it. Then again, she probably wouldn't and would just taunt him relentlessly.

"This is just what I needed, and you made it the way I like—strong, with a hint of sweetness. I could kiss you," she said, her sleep-filled voice low and throaty.

"Please do." Cole's mouth descended over hers, and he kissed her the way he planned to kiss her every morning going forward. "I have something for you," he said, reluctantly ending the kiss. He reached into the top drawer of the nightstand.

"Cole, you don't need to give me anything else. You've already done so much."

"I like giving you things and doing stuff for you, but these items are something you actually need." He handed her a set of keys to the house and a garage door opener. "You already have all of the codes. I'm thinking that we'll move you in here once you talk to Destiny."

Malaya nodded. She looked a little unsure with his last comment. Instead of telling Destiny on the phone about their plans, they both agreed that it would be better to do it in person.

That didn't mean it would be an easy conversation. He and Destiny got along great, but would she embrace him as a stepfather?

"Here's something else for you." He handed Malaya a small silver drawstring pouch.

She sat the coffee mug, keys, and remote on the nightstand closest to her and eyed Cole wearily. "What is it?"

"Open it."

After fumbling with the pouch, Malaya eventually pulled out his gift and gasped. "Oh. My. God. This is absolutely stunning," she said breathlessly.

She stared down at the electric blue crystal opal that was set in a platinum setting. The ring's wide band had an intricate design along the sides.

Cole knew it would be the perfect engagement ring.

Malaya held up the jewelry, turning it back and forth. Like Cole had done, she marveled at the way the opal glimmered under the light. "I've never seen anything like this," she said in awe.

"That's because it's one of a kind." Cole slid it on her ring finger. "I had a jeweler working on it before I first popped the question."

Malaya's head shot up and her gaze slammed into his. "But what if I said no? Actually, if you remember, I did say no. What were you going to do with the ring?"

"I would've given it to you as a friendship ring."

"Are you serious?"

Cole nodded, still holding her hand. "Months ago, I was in Miami on business and ran across this gem store. The moment I saw the stone, I thought of you. I purchased it, originally planning to have it cut into two pieces to have earrings made for your birthday, but then I thought it would look cool as a ring."

He brought her hand to his lips and kissed the back of her delicate fingers. It was something he did often, and he wasn't quite sure why.

"When the marriage idea came up, I decided why not make it into an engagement ring."

"Oh, Cole," Malaya said in a broken whisper, and tugged on the front of his T-shirt. "This is the most precious gift I have ever received in my life. Thank you, honey. I absolutely love it and will cherish it for as long as I live."

When she kissed him with so much passion, the way she was doing now, Cole felt as if he was the luckiest man on the planet. He couldn't wait to make her his wife.

CHAPTER THIRTEEN

"God, I've missed you," Malaya said, and placed a lingering kiss against her daughter's temple before hugging her tight.

"I've missed you, too, but I don't miss all of these stairs."

Malaya laughed as they walked hand in hand up to her apartment. Doing three flights of stairs every day, and sometimes twice a day, did get old after a while.

A frisson of excitement sprouted inside of her. All of this was changing soon. No more thin, dingy walls. No more loud music, thumping at all times of the night. And no more worrying about if she could make the rent. Her life was turning around for the better.

"It seems like I haven't been here in a long time," Destiny said, her cinnamon-brown skin glimmering even under the dull lights.

"I know, right? I'm so glad you're with me this weekend. A lot has happened over the last few weeks, and I can't wait to tell you everything."

The last few weeks had been a whirlwind of planning, packing, attending school, and this past week Malaya had started her new job. A job she already loved. Her whole world was coming together perfectly.

That included her relationship with Cole. They'd gotten

into a good routine and spent all of their free time together. Already, they were acting like a real couple.

We are a real couple, Malaya chastised herself.

They were getting married tomorrow and the joy ricocheting inside of her had everything to do with him. Everything about her sweetheart of a man had exceeded her expectations. She'd been so concerned about losing her independence that she had almost missed out on one of the best things that had ever happened to her.

In a short amount of time, Cole had taught her that accepting help wasn't giving up independence. It was allowing others to contribute to her life, to share their wisdom, their connections, and in some cases, their finances. There was nothing wrong with that, and it had taken a kind and generous man to show her. Having a job she loved, her own money, and a life outside of what she and Cole shared gave Malaya plenty of opportunities to flex her independence.

She unlocked the apartment door and mentally prepared herself for the conversation to come.

"Home sweet…" Destiny pulled up short just inside of the apartment, and her gaze bounced from one box to another. "Um, are you moving?"

"Yes," Malaya said.

She set Destiny's backpack and pink weekender next to the sofa. The majority of the floor space was covered with either boxes or suitcases.

"That's part of what I want to talk to you about. Come here and sit next to me."

She patted the sofa and Destiny dropped down on it, worry marring her beautiful face.

"Where are you going? You're not moving out of town, are you? Mommy, you can't." The words flew from her mouth and tears pooled in her eyes. "Is this because of Daddy?"

"Honey, calm down. As long as you're in Atlanta, I will be in Atlanta. Okay?" She ran her hand over her daughter's French braid and settled it on Destiny's back. "I'm moving for a good rea… Let's just say that this move is a good thing. A *very* good thing. I got a new job that pays well, and now I can afford a bigger place. We won't have to share a bedroom when you're visiting."

"For real? I'll have my own bedroom at your new house?" Her eyes lit up, and Malaya's pulse thumped a little faster. "Since you'll have more money, does that mean we can go to Disney World soon?"

Malaya smiled. They had taken Destiny to Disney World when she was five. That was before she fell in love with everything involving Princess Tiana. Now she wanted to return so that she could meet the princess.

"Yes, but it'll be a while. I just started the job and there's something else I need to discuss with you. First, though, what do you think of Cole?" Malaya asked, practically holding her breath for a response.

"He's great, and he's really funny. Have you ever heard him do his Kermit the Frog impression?"

"Uh, I can't say that I have."

Destiny had first met Cole one evening when Malaya had forgotten her backpack at work. He'd been gracious enough to drop it off to her and Destiny was there. Malaya had ended up inviting him to stay for dinner.

"He's funny, but not as funny as Auntie Dani."

Whenever it was Malaya's weekend to have Destiny, they usually ended up doing something with Dani on one of those days. They'd hit it off from day one.

As she listened to her daughter go on and on about Cole and Dani, she realized she had nothing to worry about. In her daughter's eyes, they were already family.

"Oh, and when Auntie Dani was yelling at Cole for buying the wrong salad dressing, I was cracking up."

Malaya laughed and wrapped her arms around her daughter's shoulders. It felt so good to hold her baby, especially after not seeing her for weeks.

"I know you have a ton of stories, but can I finish telling you my good news?" she asked.

"I thought you already did."

"I only told you half of what's going on. Not only are we moving *today*, but tomorrow...I'm getting married."

"Married!" Destiny shrieked. "*Tomorrow?*"

"Yes, I'm marrying Cole, and we're moving in with him."

Destiny's eyes went round. "For real?"

Malaya nodded and couldn't hold back her grin. Without sharing too much, she explained that she and Cole were crazy about each other and wanted to spend the rest of their lives together.

"Come with me. I want to show you something."

They headed to the bedroom and Malaya pulled out two dress bags, handing one to Destiny.

Her daughter hurried to unzip it as if she was opening a present on Christmas morning. Her sudden intake of breath was all Malaya needed to hear to know that she'd done good in picking the outfit.

"I'm going to be in your wedding?" Destiny asked, wonderment in her voice as she stared at the pale yellow and green Princess Tiana-inspired dress.

"Of course. There's no way I'd get married without you by my side. Here's my dress."

Malaya had debated on getting married in white, but Dani, her voice of reason, told her she could get married in whatever she wanted to. Cole was always saying that he liked her seventies vibe. So, she had chosen a bell-sleeved, off the shoulders, vintage seventies-style minidress with ivory lace. The outfit was cute and sexy, but also tasteful.

"That is so pretty, Mommy. Are you going to try it on? Can I try my dress on?"

"Yes, and yes, but not right now. We need to hide these back in the dress bags. Cole and some of his friends are going to be here in a little while to move all of our stuff."

"Today?" Destiny asked, and again, her eyes were huge.

Malaya laughed. Her daughter probably thought she was crazy, and maybe she was. She was crazy happy.

"I'm so excited!" Destiny shrieked, and jumped up and down with her dress hugged up against her. "This is going to be so much fun!"

"So, you're okay with me marrying Cole?"

"Yes! I knew he liked you."

"Wait. What makes you say that?" Malaya asked, surprised by the revelation.

Since being hired at Double Trouble, she'd always had a thing for Cole, and he'd asked her out plenty of times. But Malaya hadn't noticed him doing anything that would give her daughter that impression.

"Because he looks at you funny. Kinda goofy, like the way Prince Naveen looks at Princess Tiana. And Cole is really nice to you. Not like Daddy."

Her daughter started putting her princess dress back in the bag as if she hadn't just said enough to make Malaya's head explode.

Before the divorce, Malaya and Todd had tried shielding Destiny from their arguments. Even after the divorce, they made every effort not to argue in front of her; at least that was the case for Malaya. She never said anything bad about him in front of their daughter, but apparently Todd's disdain for her hadn't gone unnoticed by Destiny.

Malaya didn't know how long she stood in a trance until someone started pounding on the door.

Destiny perked up. "Do you think that's Cole and his friends?"

"Probably. Can you put my dress back in the bag while I answer the door?"

"Okay."

Malaya went to the door, still thinking about all that Destiny had said.

When she opened the door, her heart did a little giddy-up at the sight of her future husband. Always well-groomed he had gone to the barbershop earlier in the day to get his hair shaped up and his beard trimmed. Now, he stood before her looking absolutely irresistible dressed in a gray T-shirt and blue jeans that hugged his thick thighs. The single red rose in his hand only added to his dreaminess.

"For you, my gorgeous fiancée."

"*And* you're a romantic. I can't wait to find out what else I don't know about you."

"We'll have plenty of time for that, but first, show me how much you've missed me in the last eight hours."

She went willingly into his arms and they kissed as if they hadn't seen each other in months. This was something that would never get old. Some days, being with Cole still felt like a dream, but when he kissed her like this, she knew it wasn't.

He made her feel… Sexy. Desirable. Cherished.

Hearing giggling behind them was like being doused with a cold bucket of water. Cole released her and Malaya turned to see her daughter in the bedroom doorway with her hand over her mouth.

"Hey, squirt," Cole said as he walked further into the living room. "Did you hear the good news?"

"Yes, and I'm so happy," she said, giving Cole a hug like usual. "Are we getting ready to go to your house?"

"Yup, but soon it won't just be my house." He reached for Malaya and pulled her close, then draped his other arm around Destiny's shoulders. "Starting tomorrow, it will be all of ours."

Malaya lifted up on tiptoes and kissed his lips. "And I can hardly wait."

CHAPTER FOURTEEN

Cole paced the length of his home office, anxious to see Malaya. It was amazing how, in just a short amount of time, she had become such a part of him. When she wasn't by his side, he couldn't wait to see her. When she was with him, he didn't want to let her go.

Sometime between when he suggested a marriage of convenience and now, he had fallen in love with her.

Some would think that was crazy, that it was impossible to fall in love that quickly. He knew better. His parents had done it, and forty-five years later, they were even more in love. That's what he wanted with Malaya. Cole didn't know when or if she would ever love him the way he loved her, but he believed in his heart that it would happen.

He glanced at his watch for the tenth time in a matter of minutes. They were getting married in less than an hour, and Malaya and Destiny weren't there yet. They had spent the night with Dani, telling him some crap about not seeing the bride before the wedding.

"What a load of—"

"Maybe you should sit down somewhere. You're in here talking to yourself."

Cole jerked his head toward the door where Axel was

leaning against the doorjamb as if he didn't have a care in the world. He had agreed to officiate their wedding, which worked out great since they decided to get married so soon.

"Hey, you're here."

"Of course, I am. This wedding can't happen without me."

"You're right. Thanks again for officiating. I know it was last-minute."

"No problem. I'm glad I get to use my credentials again."

Axel had surprisingly gotten ordained online a year ago when a good friend of his wanted him to officiate his wedding.

"So, you ready for this?"

"I am. I can't wait to marry Malaya."

"Well, I'm glad she finally put you out of your misery. You practically stalked the woman every time you were at the bar."

Cole laughed. The guys used to tease him whenever she'd shoot down his advances.

"Is my tie straight?" he asked, referring to his bow tie. At first, they agreed that he'd just get married in a suit, but Cole had decided to go with a tuxedo. He was only getting married once; might as well look his best.

"The tie is fine."

"Did you see Malaya yet? Is she here?" Cole asked.

Axel chuckled and sat on the edge of the desk. "Man, you've got it bad. I only saw your parents, Randall and his wife, and Braxton and Londyn, which surprised me. B must be getting pretty serious about her."

Normally, the three of them met up to have a drink at Double Trouble every Friday night. It was their way of keeping up with what was going on in each other's lives. Now that they were all in relationships, they'd missed a few Fridays.

"Why do you think it's serious between Braxton and Londyn?"

"Because he brought her to a wedding. Most guys don't do that unless they're serious."

"Is that why you didn't bring Naphressa? You're not serious about her?"

"I didn't say that."

"So, you are serious about her?"

"I didn't say that either."

"Dude! For a lawyer who usually has a helluva lot to say, you ain't sayin' much."

Axel stood and shoved his hands into his pants pockets. "What's with all of the questions? Just because you found the one you want to spend the rest of your life with, doesn't mean it comes that easy for the rest of us."

"Axel, please tell me you're not still hung up on your ex."

"I didn't say that."

Cole threw up his hands. "You know what? Forget it. If you want to be evasive about NayNay, then—"

"It's Naphressa, asshole!" Axel shoved him as if they were playing one-on-one on the basketball court, and Cole burst out laughing.

"Touchy, touchy. So, you *are* feelin' this woman."

His friend huffed out a breath. "I like her, all right? It's just that we aren't at the stage of attending weddings together."

Cole nodded, but he wasn't buying it. "I hope my engagement and wedding haven't brought up too many painful memories."

"Nah, man. That was a long time ago. I'm over it." Axel had once been engaged, but his fiancée walked out on him.

"Are you, though? Are you really over it? You haven't brought Naphressa around, and I'm starting to wonder if she really exists."

"She does. Maybe I just don't want her around the likes of you," Axel said on a laugh, and then sobered. "But seriously, though. We're just hanging out right now. Nothing too serious."

Cole heard the words, but there had to be something else that was keeping him from bringing her around. He'd have to ask Dani. She'd know. She was so good at getting into everyone's business.

"All right, fellas. Let's do this," Braxton said as he hurried into the room.

"Is Malaya here?"

"Come on, man. I wouldn't have said let's do this if your woman wasn't here. She's in the downstairs guest room."

Cole rubbed his hands together. Part of him was a little nervous, but it was a good nervous. He was about to marry the woman of his dreams.

"Well, what are we waiting for? Let's do this!"

He clapped his friends on the shoulder and led the way out of his office.

*

"I'm so happy you're going to be my for-real auntie now," Malaya heard Destiny tell Dani.

The night before, when she figured out that they'd be related, her daughter lost it and fell into a fit of tears, claiming she had always wanted Dani to be her real auntie. They'd been inseparable since that moment.

They were in the attached bath in the guest room, putting the finishing touches on Destiny's hair. Malaya was leaning against the wall near the bedroom door, trying to calm her nerves. She was so emotionally overwhelmed; her heart was beating fast enough to burst out of her chest.

If that was already happening, how would she get through the wedding?

"You're not going to be sick, are you?" Dani said when she stepped out of the bathroom. "You're looking a little green around the edges."

Malaya sputtered a laugh. "I'm fine, I'm just anxious to marry your brother."

"So, you're really ready to do this, huh?"

"Beyond ready."

While talking to Cole on the phone the night before, missing him like crazy, the realization that she had fallen in love hit her like a two-by-four up against her head. She wasn't sure when it happened, but the feeling had been so staggering, she rushed him off the phone without telling him.

That won't happen again.

She planned to say *I love you* over and over again until he got sick of hearing it.

"That dress is *hot*," Dani said. "No one can pull off the seventies look the way you can. Big hair, silver jewelry, all that's missing with that outfit are white go-go boots."

"Uh, I don't think so. Then I'd look like I should be doing the bump down a soul train line." They both laughed and some of Malaya's anxiousness fell away. "What's Destiny still doing in the bathroom?"

"Putting on eye shadow and lipstick."

"What? She knows she's not allowed to wear makeup until she's sixteen." Malaya pushed away from the wall, prepared to storm the bathroom, but pulled up short.

Her daughter appeared in the doorway, looking every bit the princess in the flowing gown. It was jaw-droppingly gorgeous on her baby girl.

"Auntie Dani, this lipstick tastes good, but it's not red. It just makes my lips look wet."

Dani winked at Malaya. "That's called gloss, Niece-y-poo."

"Oh."

"*Oh* is right. It's time to get upstairs." Dani rushed around and grabbed her phone and all of their flower bouquets from the dresser. "Chop, chop. Move it. Let's go," she demanded and hurried them out of the room.

The minute Malaya saw Cole standing in the living room, a calmness that she hadn't felt all day flowed through her body. He was so handsome in the black tuxedo that molded over his muscular frame to perfection.

Cole's heated gaze scanned the length of her, and she had to keep herself from squirming under his piercing perusal. Then his eyes met hers...and he smiled. That alone had her wanting to rush through the ceremony and get right to the honeymoon.

Instead of standing where he'd been instructed to stand in front of Axel and next to Braxton, Cole headed her way. He always complained about Dani not following directions and doing whatever she wanted, but they were two of a kind.

Malaya didn't mind in this case. She wanted to leap into his arms and hold on tight.

But she wouldn't.

At least not yet.

"Damn, baby. You look *good*." He slid his arm around her waist and gave her a quick kiss before leaning in close. "That dress is slammin' but I can't wait to get it off of you and get a taste of what's hidden beneath."

Heat rose to Malaya's cheeks. She didn't dare glance around the room. She could already feel everyone's attention on them.

Cole escorted her into the living room and they stopped in front of Axel, who nodded a greeting. As he started the ceremony, Malaya and Cole exchanged heated glances. The moment seemed so surreal. Had someone told her a year ago that she would be marrying him, she would've laughed them out of the room. Yet, here she was.

"Cole and Malaya have written their own vows," Axel said, and nodded for Cole to begin.

When he reached to hold both of her hands, Malaya hurried to give her bouquet to Dani. When she turned back to him, they stood face to face, staring into each other's eyes.

"Malaya Antoinette Radcliff, from the first day I met you, I knew I wanted you in my life. Even though you shot me down more times than I can count—" they both laughed, "— I am so glad you finally gave me a chance. You are the most resilient woman I have ever met. I look forward to watching you soar to even higher levels. I will always support your dreams and desires. I will take care of you when you're sick, and comfort you when you're sad. I promise to love you, protect you, provide for you, and be that irresistible husband you've always dreamed of having."

Dani snorted. "Oh, Lord."

Cole glared at his sister. "*Anyway*, as I was saying. I make this promise before God, my family, and our friends."

Malaya's hand shook as he slid the engagement ring, along with a platinum band, onto her finger. He then placed a lingering kiss on the back of her hand. It was his thing, something he did often, and she had to hold back a giggle since his beard tickled.

"Malaya," Axel prompted.

"Colton James Eubanks, I can't wait to be your wife. I might've turned down your advances, but it wasn't because I wasn't interested. I have admired you from afar. Now that I've gotten to know you, I'm awed by your character, your generosity, and your kindness. You make me feel as if I'm the most important person in your world. Thank you for always being there for me, supporting me, and encouraging me to live my best life. More importantly, thank you for being my friend. *I love you.*"

She emphasized those three words, wanting to make sure he heard them. His brows inched up and the sexy grin that she'd fallen in love with spread across his mouth.

"You have shown me how a real man treats a woman," she continued. "Today, I am promising to *love you*, respect you, and cherish you all the days of my life. Oh, and I'll allow you to be the head of our household." Everyone laughed. "I make this promise before God, our family, and our friends."

She slid the platinum band that was similar to hers onto his ring finger. Then, staring into his eyes, she brought his hand to her lips and kissed the back of it. He shivered in her hold and her lips twitched, trying to keep from laughing.

"I love you," she repeated.

"Alrighty then," Axel said in amusement. "On that note, by the power invested in me, I now pronounce you husband and wife. Cole, you may kiss your bride."

"Finally. Come here, Mrs. Eubanks."

Cole covered her mouth with his and Malaya practically melted when his lips touched hers.

They did it. They were now husband and wife, and she was ready to shout it to the world.

CHAPTER FIFTEEN

"Ohhh, dang. Did you see that?" Braxton yelled. "David elbowed Lebron in the jaw, and he's getting away with it."

After missing several Friday meetups at Double Trouble, Axel suggested that he, Braxton, and Cole hook up to watch a Lakers game. Cole volunteered to host, and Malaya prepared a spread that would normally be reserved for Super Bowl Sunday.

As if just thinking about her could conjure her up, Cole's phone dinged three times, signaling a text from his wife.

My wife.

They'd been married for weeks and still he got the feels whenever he referred to her as his *wife*. He grabbed the phone from the side table next to the sofa and glanced at the screen.

Malaya: *I can't stop thinking about last night. I want a repeat.*

Cole grinned. The night before, he learned that his wife had a freaky side. He had no problem rising to the occasion.

Cole: *Anything you want, baby. Hurry home, and I'll kick the fellas out.*

Malaya: *We'll start in the kitchen and work our way through the house. Oh, I'll only be wearing my wedding ring.*

Cole: *Damn. I love it when you talk dirty. I'm 'bout to kick these brothas out now!*

"That must be Laya. Your butt over there grinning like a

coyote eating a thick, juicy ribeye," Braxton cracked and they all laughed.

"Don't hate, man. I'm sure if Londyn called, you would be running up out of here to get to her. And Axel—"

"Don't start with me. Just get the door and be quiet," he said when the doorbell rang.

Cole glanced out the living room window and growled under his breath when he saw it was Todd. His pompous ass wasn't supposed to be there to pick up Destiny for another couple of hours.

They'd finally met the day after the wedding, and Cole immediately didn't like the arrogant jerk. Malaya insisted that he wasn't always like that, but that superior attitude was probably always present.

The doorbell rang again.

Axel narrowed his eyes. "Tell me that's not one of your exes."

"Of course not. That's Destiny's father."

Braxton snorted. "So what? You gon' pretend you ain't here and leave him out there? He can't be that bad."

"He is."

For Destiny's and Malaya's sake, Cole always tried to be civil, but they weren't there. If he let the guy in, he didn't know if he could be nice to the man.

The bell rang again, and he lunged from his seat.

"Take a breath, man. Take a breath," Axel warned.

Cole swung the door open. "What's up, Todd? Destiny isn't here yet."

"What? I told Malaya I was picking Destiny up early. She said that she'd be here."

"Oh, if that's the case, I'm sure they're on their way." They had gone to visit Mrs. Patterson, something Malaya did weekly since moving away from her old neighbor. "Do you want to come in? Or you waitin' out there?"

Todd huffed out a loud breath. "I guess I'll come in."

He strolled into the house with his chest puffed out as if he was the king of the free world. Cole hated people like him.

People who had a little money and thought everyone should kiss their feet.

Axel and Braxton stood.

"Guys, this is Destiny's father, Todd Stapleton. Todd, this is Axel Becker and Braxton Harper."

The men nodded, but no one moved to shake hands. Cole couldn't much blame his buddies. The vibe Todd was giving off would've turned off a saint.

"Have a seat. We were just watching the game."

Cole reclaimed his seat on the sofa. "Do you want something to eat or drink?" he asked as an afterthought, noting that Todd was checking out the place.

"No. I'm good." He roamed around the space and stopped near the mantle and eyed the photos. Then turned back to Cole. "This is what you do on Sundays? Sit around, eat, and drink. I'd think you'd be out with your wife and my daughter, doing family stuff. How else are you going to make this marriage look like something other than the farce that it is?"

"*Ah, shit,*" Braxton murmured.

Cole stood slowly, trying to stay calm. "You know, it would probably be better if you waited outside."

"I prefer to wait in here."

"Cole," Axel said slowly, warning in his tone.

Todd's tone was so snobbish, annoyance clawed at Cole, and he hadn't realized he moved toward the guy. Axel's legal brain was undoubtedly already coming up with a defense that could help keep him out of jail.

"Todd, maybe you *should* wait for Malaya and Destiny outside," Braxton reasoned, standing in front of Cole, as if that would keep him from pummeling the arrogant ass.

"Why? Does the truth hurt?" Todd taunted and moved closer. "Do you think I don't know you two got married to improve Malaya's chances in court against me?"

Cole said nothing. Clearly, the man was itching for a fight, and that's the last thing Cole wanted.

"Nothing to say, huh? You can't honestly expect me to

believe that you married Malaya for any other reason. She's like a bloodsucking—"

"Get the hell out of my house!" Cole charged at him, but Braxton caught him around the waist. "Let me go, B! I want him out of my house. 'Cause what he ain't gon' do is stand in front of me and disrespect my wife!"

"I'm not going anywhere, and if you put your hands on me, I will slap you with a lawsuit so fast it'll make your head spin."

"What's going on here?"

Cole jerked his head toward the stairs where Malaya and Destiny were standing.

"I told you I was on my way! Where the hell have you been with my daughter?" Todd snapped.

Malaya got in his face. "First of all, don't talk to me like that. Secondly, I told you we were on our way. It's not my fault you beat us here." She turned to Destiny who remained near the stairs, her eyes wide with shock. "Honey, go upstairs and get your bag."

"Okay," she said and took off.

Malaya approached Cole. *Sorry about him,* she mouthed before kissing him. He loved his wife and her kisses more than anything, but neither stopped him from wanting to choke the hell out of her ex.

Except for the television, silence filled the space and he could cut the tension with a chainsaw. Cole wouldn't relax until the man was out of his house.

"Destiny, hurry up," Todd yelled with impatience, and started pacing the floor like a caged animal. "Let's go. Now!"

"Okaaay, I'm coming." Seconds later, Destiny was back. "Mommy, did you see my yellow—"

"I said let's go!" Todd yanked on her arm and pulled her toward the door.

Son of...

Cole charged forward and slammed him against the wall. "If you ever put your hands on her again, I will ki—"

"You will what?" Todd goaded, an evil sneer marring his

face. "Whatchu gon' do?"

"Daddy, don't say that. I'm ready. We can leave."

Malaya tugged on Cole's arm. "Honey, please let him go. He's not worth it."

Cole started to back away, but Todd swung at him. Missed.

Before Cole could stop himself, he slammed his fist into the man's jaw, and watched him drop to the floor as if a hundred-pound dumbbell was tied to his neck.

Destiny screamed.

Axel cursed.

Malaya gasped. "Oh, dear God. What have you done?"

*

Malaya paced back and forth in the master bedroom, getting angrier with each step she took. She'd been up there for ten minutes, unable to believe what Cole had done. What type of example was he setting for her child? That it was okay to punch people when they say something he didn't like?

A soft knock sounded on the door. "Mommy? Can I come in?"

Malaya's heart kicked inside of her chest, surprised to hear Destiny's voice. She had left with Todd before Malaya had stormed up the stairs. Or so she thought.

She hurried to the door and swung it open. Destiny stood there, nervously rocking from one foot to the other and holding a bottle of water.

"Cole told me to give you this." She handed Malaya the water. "And this." She pulled her hand from around her back and opened it. There was a heart-shaped piece of chocolate wrapped in red foil sitting in her palm.

Malaya's heart fluttered. "That man." She was definitely a goner if a piece of chocolate made her love him even more.

"Can I come in?" Destiny asked again.

"Of course, honey. I'm so sorry for what happened downstairs." She wrapped her arm around her daughter and guided her to the bench at the foot of the bed. "Where's your dad? I thought you guys left."

"We did, but I talked to him," she said, sounding like she was thirty instead of ten. "He knows he messed up."

"Does he?"

"Yes. He said he overreacted and that he didn't mean to grab me like that."

"Has he put his hands on you before?"

Destiny shook her head. "No. He's never acted like that before. I don't think he likes Cole, but that's okay. I don't think Cole likes him that much, either."

Malaya sat speechless. Her child was wise beyond her years. "Why do you say that?"

"I just have a feeling, but Cole tries to be nice to him because of me."

Malaya hugged her tight. "Oh, sweetheart. I hope what Cole did doesn't change your opinion of him. He doesn't usually behave like that."

"I know. He told me he didn't like the way Daddy talked to you and grabbed on me. He's real protective of us."

Malaya laughed. "Yes, he is. That's because he loves us very much. He doesn't want anyone ever disrespecting either of us."

"I know. Are you mad at him?"

"I was. I understood why he hit your father, but hitting people because they say or do something you don't like is never okay. Understand?"

"Yes."

"Mommy, are you and Cole getting a divorce?"

The sincerity in her daughter's eyes and the innocence of the question caused Malaya's world to teeter.

Guilt had plagued her for years after her and Todd's divorce. She had always questioned what she could've done differently to keep her family together. No parent wanted to drag their child through a divorce.

"No, honey. I love Cole with all my heart. Even if he made me angry, we're not getting a divorce."

"But you and Daddy did."

"I know, but...but that was different. Your father and I

grew apart, and we couldn't fix what was broken in our relationship. We were making each other miserable. That's why we had to get a divorce. It's different with Cole."

"How?"

"How is it different?"

Destiny bobbed her head up and down, her braids bouncing back and forth.

How is it different? Malaya asked herself.

"Well, for one thing, Cole loves me unconditionally."

"What does that mean?"

"It means that even if I do something he doesn't like, he doesn't stop loving me."

"Oh."

"And Cole...he's sweet, and he's kind, and like you said, he's funny. We do a lot of laughing, and he makes me so happy. Kinda like you do." Malaya bumped shoulders with her daughter, causing Destiny to giggle. "I'm planning to spend the rest of my life with him."

"I'm glad because he told me I can call him Dad."

"He did?"

"Yeah. Yesterday, I asked if I could because...because he's just like a dad."

Cole hadn't mentioned the conversation to Malaya. "What did he say?"

"At first he looked at me funny, like he was going to cry."

Malaya's lips twitched, but she fought the urge to laugh. She was pretty sure she knew what expression her daughter was referring to. It was the same one Cole had when they were exchanging their wedding vows.

"Then he said, that would be cool. Now I have a daddy and a dad," Destiny said proudly and tears pricked the back of Malaya's eyes.

Her daughter was growing up too fast. It seemed like only yesterday she was learning how to talk. Now she was coming into her own, figuring out what she wanted, and going after it.

"That was nice of you to ask him."

"I'm glad I did. I think I made him happy."

Malaya nodded and took a long swig of her water.

"I think Cole wants a baby," Destiny blurted.

Water spewed from Malaya's mouth. "What?" she croaked, and coughed a few times when some of the liquid went down the wrong way.

Destiny giggled. "That was funny. Water flew all the way to the other side of the room. I think some got on the mirror."

"Never mind the mirror. What are you talking about? What makes you think Cole wants a baby? Wait." Malaya studied her daughter, noting she was looking everywhere but at her. "Is it Cole or is this you petitioning for one?"

"I was thinking that since Daddy and Selena didn't give me a sister or a brother, can you and Cole give me one?"

"I love that idea."

Malaya and Destiny jumped at the sound of Cole's deep voice.

"See, Mommy? I told you. Dad wants a baby, too."

Malaya shook her head, not bothering to respond. She already knew where Cole stood on the subject.

"Destiny, sweetheart, can I speak to your mommy for a minute? Oh, and your father said you can stay with us another night."

She leaped up and did a fist pump. Something she'd seen Cole do on more than one occasion. "Yes!"

When Destiny left, Malaya glanced at Cole, who was grinning like a proud papa. "She's growing up way too fast."

"She's a great kid." Cole sat on the bench next to Malaya. He was leaned forward with his elbows on his thighs and his hands clasped in front of him. "I'm sorry," he said, staring down at his hands.

"Yeah, me, too," she said.

"Todd is an asshole," Cole continued. "However, I still should've had more control. When he grabbed Destiny…I just lost it. I don't know what came over me."

"It's what parents do when they think their child is in danger. Todd is a jerk most of the time, but he has never been physically abusive to me or Destiny. Impatient? Yes. A know-it-all? Absolutely. An asshole? Most definitely. But he has never and would never cause us physical harm."

"Yeah, he did seem a little shaken up, and not because I popped him. When he came back to the house with Destiny, we talked for a minute and came to an understanding."

"I'm shocked."

"I was, too."

"Cole, you're a former boxer, and let Dani tell it, your hands are lethal weapons. You could've killed him."

"I know, baby, and knowing that scared me. It won't happen again. I never want to do anything to hurt you, Destiny, or your chances of getting full custody of her.

"When he was on that floor, all I could think about was if I go to prison, who would take care of you and Destiny."

"Oh, honey." Malaya looped her arm through his and rested her head on his shoulder. "I know he said he was pressing charges, but if he came back and dropped Destiny off, it's safe to say that's not going to happen."

"Yeah, he said as much, but I still feel bad about the whole situation. Can you ever forgive me?"

Malaya lifted her head and stared into her man's eyes. "You came to me and my child's defense. There's nothing to forgive. Just promise me you won't make beating up on folks a habit."

He chuckled. "Deal, but when Destiny starts dating assholes, the deal is off."

"Uh, that's the last thing I want to think about, but okay. I can live with that."

Cole leaned over and kissed her. "I love you, sweetheart."

"Not as much as I love you."

EPILOGUE

Nineteen months later...

Malaya stood in the doorway of the nursery, quietly watching Cole change six-month-old CJ's diaper. Observing him whenever he was with their kids never got old. She couldn't have asked for a better father for them.

Married almost a year and a half, Cole had turned out to be more than she could have ever dreamed. He truly was an irresistible husband who showed her daily what it meant to love unconditionally.

So much had happened in their life together. Months after they were married, she graduated with her business degree. That same week, she made amends with her parents and also found out she was pregnant. To say it had been an emotional week would be an understatement.

"Mommy," Destiny called up the stairs, and Malaya glanced down the hall just when she came into view. "Auntie Dani's on the phone. She wants to know what time she should be here tomorrow, and she said don't even think about leaving her."

Malaya laughed. They were taking their second trip to Disney World, and to Destiny's delight, Dani insisted on tagging along.

"I'm not sure. Ask your dad."

"Okay. Hold on, Auntie Dani." Destiny strolled into the room with the phone plastered to her ear. "Dad…"

Malaya smiled as they discussed the plans. Her life had turned into a fairytale.

After Cole and Todd's altercation, she went to court regarding custody. She had been cautiously optimistic that the judge would rule in her favor, especially since Destiny would get a say. After the judge listened to the case and talked with Destiny, Malaya was awarded physical custody. Todd didn't fight that or the joint custody ruling, saying that all he wanted was for his daughter to be happy.

Though he and Cole tolerated each other, there still was no love between them. But they both put on a good front for their daughter's sake.

"You look as if you're a hundred miles away," Cole said as he approached her. "What's on your mind?"

Malaya glanced over his shoulder to where Destiny was reading to CJ, and the baby was looking as if understood every word she was saying. "She's a great big sister."

"Yes, she is." Cole slipped his arm around Malaya's waist and nuzzled the erogenous spot behind her ear. "Destiny is petitioning for a baby sister."

Malaya laughed as he quietly guided her into the hallway and backed her against a wall. Her eyes drifted shut and desire invaded her body as the sweet assault of his lips on her neck had her pulse racing.

"Mmm," she moaned. "You don't play fair when you and Destiny gang up on me about babies. You're impossible to resist when you torture me like this."

"That's all I needed to hear."

Malaya squeaked, then burst out laughing when he suddenly scooped her into his arms and headed down the hall.

"Where are we going?"

"I want to show you something in our bedroom."

"I bet you do, but if this is about making a baby, I think

two is enough."

"Yeah, you say that now, but I have my ways of changing your mind."

"Oh, really?" Malaya grinned, knowing he could talk her into almost anything. "In that case, show me."

*

If you enjoyed this book by Sharon C. Cooper,
Please consider leaving a review on Amazon, review sites or social media
outlets.

*

Also, learn more about Supreme Security—where Malaya was recently hired—by checking out my *Atlanta's Finest* series!

*

Don't forget to grab the other books in the Irresistible Husband Series.

DO ME by Sheryl Lister
LOVE ME by Delaney Diamond

Join Sharon's Mailing List

To get sneak peeks of upcoming stories and to hear about giveaways that Sharon is sponsoring, go to https://sharoncooper.net/newsletter to join her mailing list.

About the Author

Award-winning and bestselling author, Sharon C. Cooper, is a romance-a-holic - loving anything that involves romance with a happily-ever-after, whether in books, movies, or real life. Sharon writes contemporary romance, as well as romantic suspense and enjoys rainy days, carpet picnics, and peanut butter and jelly sandwiches. She's been nominated for numerous awards and is the recipient of Emma Awards (RSJ) for Author of the Year 2019, Favorite Hero 2019 (INDEBTED), Romantic Suspense of the Year 2015 (TRUTH OR CONSEQUENCES), Interracial Romance of the Year 2015 (ALL YOU'LL EVER NEED), and BRAB (book club) Award -Breakout Author of the Year 2014. When Sharon isn't writing, she's hanging out with her amazing husband, doing volunteer work or reading a good book (a romance of course). To read more about Sharon and her novels, visit www.sharoncooper.net

Website: https://sharoncooper.net
Join Sharon's mailing list: https://bit.ly/31Xsm36
Facebook fan page:
http://www.facebook.com/AuthorSharonCCooper21?ref=hl
Twitter: https://twitter.com/#!/Sharon_Cooper1
Subscribe to her blog:
http://sharonccooper.wordpress.com/
Goodreads:
http://www.goodreads.com/author/show/5823574.Sharon_C_Cooper
Pinterest: https://www.pinterest.com/sharonccooper/
Instagram:
https://www.instagram.com/authorsharonccooper/

Other Titles

Atlanta's Finest Series

A Passionate Kiss (book 1- prequel)

Vindicated (book 2)

Indebted (book 3)

Accused (book 4)

Betrayed (book 5)

Hunted (book 6) – Coming Soon

Jenkins & Sons Construction Series (Contemporary Romance)

Love Under Contract (book 1)

Proposal for Love (book 2)

A Lesson on Love (book 3)

Unplanned Love (book 4)

Jenkins Family Series (Contemporary Romance)

Best Woman for the Job (Short Story Prequel)

Still the Best Woman for the Job (book 1)

All You'll Ever Need (book 2)

Tempting the Artist (book 3)

Negotiating for Love (book 4)

Seducing the Boss Lady (book 5)

Love at Last (Holiday Novella)

When Love Calls (Novella)

More Than Love (Novella)

Reunited Series (Romantic Suspense)

Blue Roses (book 1)

Secret Rendezvous (Prequel to Rendezvous with Danger)

Rendezvous with Danger (book 2)

Truth or Consequences (book 3)

Operation Midnight (book 4)

Stand Alones

Something New ("Edgy" Sweet Romance)

Legal Seduction (Harlequin Kimani – Contemporary Romance)

Sin City Temptation (Harlequin Kimani – Contemporary Romance)

A Dose of Passion (Harlequin Kimani – Contemporary Romance)

Model Attraction (Harlequin Kimani – Contemporary Romance)

Soul's Desire (Contemporary Romance)

Show Me (Contemporary Romance)

Show Me

Made in the USA
Columbia, SC
27 April 2021

36956802R00078